Sunspot

Dear Jackie

Enjoy!

Frederick Musser

11/25/09

By
Frederick Musser

PublishAmerica
Baltimore

© 2008 by Frederick Musser.
All rights reserved. No part of this book may be reproduced, stored in a retrieval system or transmitted in any form or by any means without the prior written permission of the publishers, except by a reviewer who may quote brief passages in a review to be printed in a newspaper, magazine or journal.

First printing

All characters in this book are fictitious, and any resemblance to real persons, living or dead, is coincidental.

ISBN: 1-60474-598-3
PUBLISHED BY PUBLISHAMERICA, LLLP
www.publishamerica.com
Baltimore

Printed in the United States of America

Sunspot

Chapter 1

Waves of heat danced up from the blacktop to distort the view of the horizon. The shallow breathing of the man was all that could be heard in the quiet heat of the day. A thick slime of sweat and dust clung to him, which acted like a sunscreen, preventing his sunburned skin from being damaged more. He had no way of knowing how long he had been wandering, but he was certain that if he did not get some water or medical attention soon, he would surely perish.

The late afternoon sun soon gave way to the haze of dusk as he continued to press on. It grew dark and the cool breeze felt good, giving him added strength. He looked around and tried to focus on the distant horizon for some sign of civilization but found none. He looked to the stars, some brighter than others, and he realized the immenseness of the night sky was dizzying. His only hope was that he was on a road and sooner or later someone would pass by. He fixed his gaze on two of the stars that seemed brighter than the others and were straight ahead of him. As he walked on, he realized that they were not stars at all but instead, headlights of an approaching vehicle. His heart began to beat more rapidly, and he grew excited as the anticipation of his rescue took hold. Larger and larger, the two circles of light grew closer and closer. The man began to wave his arms back and forth. He tried to yell for attention but his throat was so dry that nothing came out. His mind was racing as he tried to think of what he would do if the vehicle didn't stop. He suddenly felt dizzy and his legs would not obey the commands given. Then a new fear arose that he would be run over before he was seen. He could now hear the sound of the engine as the vehicle bore down on him, and he knew if he didn't get out of the way, nothing that happened till now would matter. The brightness of the headlights was blinding, and he suddenly felt as if all time had stopped. And then, just as if a large hole had opened up and swallowed his world…blackness…quiet…blackness.

Dr. Alex Trumbull sat at his desk shuffling several papers, making notations on some and completely ignoring others. Since being promoted to department head of the neurological studies at Las Vegas Memorial Hospital, it seemed he had time for little else. Dr. Al, as his friends called him, had been practicing in his chosen field for some twenty-five years before his calling to be department head. He always thought of himself as some hands-on type of guy, and so this new position was uncomfortable. In his office far removed from doctor-patient interaction, he felt somewhat useless. Placing his favorite coffee cup down at the edge of his modern desk, he got up out of the leather high-back chair and slowly walked toward his office door. He almost made it when the sound of his phone stopped him.

"Hello!"

"Good morning, Al. It's Ted. How are you?"

"Oh, I'm fine. I was just going over the latest reports from your ward and decided that I needed a second cup of coffee to get me through. You caught me as I was leaving. What's up?" Al asked as he lowered his large frame to his desk top.

"Well, don't sound so mundane. I told you when you took that promotion that would happen."

"Does it show that much?" Al asked.

"Only to those who know you, buddy. Listen. I wanted to know if you're free for golf tomorrow. I've been practicing with this new set of clubs Helen bought me for my birthday, and I'd swear they've helped me shave ten points off my score."

"Tomorrow? Hell, why not today?" Al said with all the eagerness of a child waiting to open presents on Christmas. "I could really use some fresh air and sunshine."

"I can't today, Al. I have a post-op conference scheduled for two, and besides, I'm waiting for some test results on a patient that I've been meaning to discuss with you. It's a real interesting case. A truck driver brought a man in from the desert suffering from exposure. It seems he was wandering out there, completely naked. Scared the driver silly when he collapsed in front of his truck and he had to swerve off the road to avoid hitting him."

Al stood up. "Well, I guess it's tomorrow then," he said, trying to hide his disappointment and not even questioning Ted further on the patient. "I'll meet you at the clubhouse by the first hole."

The two doctors hung up and Al went for his second cup of coffee. As he walked the corridor to the elevator, the thought of having an interesting case to be involved in gave him new energy.

It was four a.m. the next day when the phone rang. On about the sixth ring, Dr. Trumbull turned to answer it.

"Hello!" Al said as he tried to clear the cobwebs from his head and the frog from his throat.

"Hi, Al, it's Ted. I'm sorry to call you at this hour, but I'm down at the hospital and I need to see you as soon as possible."

"What's the urgency?" Al tried to focus his eyes on the clock on his night stand. "At four a.m."

"Remember that case I mentioned on the phone? The guy from the desert?"

"Oh, yes, the interesting one."

"Well, it just got more interesting. In fact, it's more than that; it's downright scary."

"Is this the same Ted I know who goes skydiving and then camping in the mountains with all kinds of wild animals, and then hikes his way out and calls it a vacation?"

"I'm serious, Al. Things are happening with this patient that I can't find a reason for. I'm in the isolation ward on two south. Come in the rear entrance, and don't tell anyone you see why you're there. I'll meet you in the conference room."

"Okay, give me about a half hour," Al said. He hung up and rose from the comfort of his bed to the cold of the shower. He thought it might be a long day, and he liked to be as fresh as he could. As he dressed, he thought about the tone of Ted's voice. He never heard him sound so unsure of himself, and to have a patient in the isolation ward usually meant that a doctor was losing control of the situation, something that normally doesn't happen to Ted.

The drive to the hospital was as uneventful as the lives of most people at this hour of the day; not much traffic and the weather was clear. Al parked his car in the rear lot and walked to the service entrance. The door was locked and after tapping on it, the guard, seeing a familiar face, came and greeted him.

"Good morning, Doc. You're in a little early, huh?"

"Hi, Pete. Yeah, I have some special work I have to take care of in the labs, and I figured to park back here to be closer to my car in case it rains."

Al walked past Pete, who looked at the doctor with a wrinkled brow as he stared up at the still early morning sky. Not a cloud was visible. Al then realized what he said and hoped Pete didn't notice. He never was much good at lying, even casually. Al didn't look back. He knew it was pointless to correct what he said. Pete was a retired cop of some twenty-eight years and Al was sure he knew he lied.

"Have a good day, Doc!" Pete's voice trailed away as Al turned the first corner he came to just to get out of view.

The isolation ward of the hospital was the newest wing. It hosted all the latest equipment for almost any type of medical problem. Dr. Trumbull was proud to be associated with such an establishment. He missed working on the wards and having all the best in technology at his disposal. Most of all, he missed the people he worked with. Just as he started to reminisce in his mind, the door to the conference room at the end of the hall opened and he could see Ted wave to him. As Al got closer, he tried to get a read of Ted's face without success.

"I'm glad you came down," Ted started. "Come on in, I want to show you the latest reports that I have."

The two of them sat down at a table across from each other as Ted continued.

"The patient has given his name as Mike Conners. He says that he can't recall why he was wandering around in the desert, as much of his memory is still unclear, and when he first woke up, he was barely able to give us that. As you can see by some of the preliminary tests I ran on him, he was suffering from exposure and dehydration. Also he had severe burns on his hands."

"Maybe he was in a car accident which caught fire and he pulled himself out," Al said.

"I thought of that. I guess we won't really know until his memory improves. Anyway, that's about as normal as this case gets, because from there it goes downhill. When he was first brought in, he was unconscious and so we performed the usual activity to stabilize him. After that he was hooked up to the encephalograph to monitor his brain activity," Ted continued as he handed the reports to Al. "As you can see, the readings that we got were not those of an unconscious subject, but one of someone quite awake and, in fact, they fluctuate right off the scale."

"Maybe these readings were caused in part by the medication he was given," Al said as he continued to study the report.

"That had occurred to me also. But you can see by the later reports that we got just about the same readings when I changed the medication and used a different encephalograph. And as if that's not enough…" Ted's' voice trailed off.

"Okay, Ted, what do you mean by 'enough' and what else is there that has you scared?" Al stared at Ted, whose face took on a look that could only be characterized as a person in denial of what he knew.

"I guess the best way for you to understand is to see for yourself," Ted said as he motioned for Al to follow him. The two of them left the conference room and walked past the night nurse who was stationed at her console monitoring the equipment connected to Mike Conners' room.

"Any change?" Ted asked

"No, Doctor."

Mike Conners' room was at the very end of the corridor, and the door faced the two doctors as they walked. The hallway was somewhat dimly lit and as they got closer, a blue-green light could be seen coming from under the door.

Ted walked a few steps in front of Al and opened the door first with his back to it. As Al walked through the doorway he noticed the blue-green light filled the whole room. He glanced around quickly to find the source to be coming from the area of Mike

Conners' bed. He didn't see any lamps, and for several seconds his own brain couldn't seem to comprehend what his eyes were showing him. The source of the light was not coming from any manmade appliance such as a lamp or other medical equipment, but rather from the patient himself.

"Incredible!" was the first word Dr. Trumbull could muster. "Absolutely incredible."

Ted motioned for Al to go take a closer look as he stayed by the door. Al took a few steps toward the bed, his curiosity welling up inside and his mind trying to make some sense of all of this. As he got closer, he noticed a strange feeling start to take hold and a numbing sensation, along with a feeling that everything was slowing down. Fear intruded on his curiosity, and he found himself retreating to the safety of the door where Ted stood.

"What was that I felt?" Al said as Ted reached for his arm to steady him. "I felt like everything was slowing down and I was inside a room full of jello." Ted nodded in agreement.

"I had the same experience myself, right before I called you. Scared me too. After watching you, well, at least I know I'm not crazy. I think it's some form of protection that Mr. Conners is able to use while he sleeps. The funny thing is that it doesn't always occur."

"Self-protection!" Al repeated. "Protection from what? And for what purpose?"

"I'm not sure, but it only seems to happen during phases of REM sleep, the deepest sleep when the body does the most recharging, after which it fades away."

"Well, I can certainly see why you called me. I guess we'll have to wait for Mr. Conners to wake up and hope more of his memory returns to help shed some more light on this, no pun intended."

The two doctors left the room and walked back past the

attending nurse. Ted glanced her way and then waited for her to look up.

"Call me a soon as Mr. Conners wakes up."

"Yes, Doctor."

"She's the only other medical staff member who knows of this, and I'd like to keep it that way, Al." Al stopped and turned to face Ted.

"That's OK with me. The only other problem is that I'm sure you're aware of hospital policy pertaining to unidentified patients." Ted let out a slow, low sigh.

"If you mean notifying the local authorities, I already have."

"Good, for all we know we could be harboring some mass murderer, which wouldn't sit well with the medical review board, if you know what I mean."

Ted nodded in agreement.

Chapter 2

It was ten o'clock in the morning when the dark blue van stopped in front of 26 Carter Lane. The tall man dressed in green coveralls exited and stretched as he walked to the rear and opened the doors. The bright sun had warmed the morning air and it felt relaxing to him. It was early summer and several children rode their bikes past him as he took the basket of flowers in one hand and a clipboard in the other. He walked up the driveway and looked around to see if anyone else noticed him. He thought how nice this place was. All the lawns were well-manicured and the streets clean. It must be nice to live here and maybe raise a family. He would love to be able to have the time for such things, and he knew someday he would force himself to do just that. As for now, his priorities were elsewhere. He reached for the doorbell and pressed. Turning his back once more to look around the streets, he waited for a reply. The front door opened and Melissa Conners looked out to see the man turn towards her and smile. She smiled back.

"Good morning, come on in," she said as she backed up to make room for him.

"Here, these are for you." He thrust out the flowers and hoped she would take them quickly as it made him feel uncomfortable. There was something about this disguise that didn't sit well with Phil Grant. He was a strong-minded agent who always took his job seriously.

"Well, thank you, Mr. Grant. I must say this identity you have today is better than that plumber you impersonated last time."

She was clearly having fun with him, which under the circumstances made him feel even worse. He tried to ignore it all and went on.

"Well, I received your request for a meeting and got here as soon as I could. Has he tried to contact you?"

"No, I was hoping you had heard something." She did not give him time to talk. "It's been four months since Mike disappeared and I go on day after day not know what to think. If he's dead then I wish someone would tell me so I could get on with my life." She sighed and sank down on the sofa. Her petite frame hardly dented the cushions and her long blond hair looked lighter than normal against the black leather upholstery. Agent Grant stepped behind the coffee table but didn't sit down.

"I wish I had something to tell you, Mrs. Conners, but I don't." He opened his mouth to say something else but she cut him off.

"And another thing, I'm tired of being cooped up in this house. It's a beautiful place, don't get me wrong, it's even nicer than the first house we stayed at." She shifted her weight as to get more comfortable and continued.

"Which leads me to wonder if and when Mike does show up, how is he going to know where to find me?" She didn't wait for an answer. "I need to get away somewhere. This government witness protection program feels more like a prison sentence than a new life, and besides, I miss my old life, my family and friends."

She was clearly frustrated and Agent Grant felt obliged to let her vent; after all he felt partially responsible for her husband's disappearance since he was in charge of their protection. Not wanting to seem like an authority figure but friend, he sat down on the tufted chair across from her.

"Look, I never said it would be easy. When Mike disappeared, as you know, we had to move you for your own good to this house because we didn't know if the people Mike testified against had anything to do with his disappearance. We try to make things as comfortable as possible for you. We have to be extra careful due to the kinds of people that could go after you and Mike. And when the time comes, I will personally bring Mike to you. We have agents watching your old house around the clock. If you feel you have to get away for a while, then let me see what I can arrange for you."

He attempted to get up, but noticed the swelling of tears in Melissa's eyes and sat back down. "I understand how frustrating this must be for you, and I can assure you I've checked out every lead I could come up with on this." He clasped his hands between his legs and looked down at the plush green rug between his feet. "I really feel Mike is out there somewhere." His voice trailed away at the end of his sentence. The room seemed suddenly uncomfortably quiet and Phil sensed it was time to leave. He stood up and turned to walk toward the door. Melissa got up also.

"I'm sorry, Agent Grant. I didn't mean to dump on you like that." Phil Grant looked at her and thought of how special she was, and nice on the eyes also. If he was Mike Conners he certainly wouldn't want to be away for too long.

"That's OK, Mrs. Conners, I'll let myself out." He started walking toward the door when he remembered his clipboard that he placed on the coffee table and went back to retrieve it.

"I wouldn't want to forget this," Phil said. As he bent over to pick it up, his cell phone started to ring. Placing the clipboard back down, he straightened to get the phone out of his inner overall pocket.

"Yes." A long moment of silence found Phil and Melissa staring into each other's eyes. Melissa, who had stopped crying, was trying to be polite and not seem nosy but her curiosity wouldn't let her stop her attentive stare.

"Okay, I understand. No, I can't. Yes." Phil hung up.

"What is it?" Melissa asked.

"Nothing to worry about. Just my office keeping tabs on me."

He moved more quickly now, trying to make his escape before Melissa had a chance to question him further about the phone call. "Like I said, give me some time to find out about a change of scenery for you."

"Alright, but don't let me wait too long." She got up and walked Phil to the door. She was still curious about that phone call but wouldn't press further.

Phil was two miles from the house when he pulled off the road to re-contact his office.

"Hello, Alice, it's Phil. Sorry but I couldn't talk before. So where you sending me? Vegas! I haven't been there in years."

Phil switched ears. "Who do I contact there? Okay, good."

The secretary on the other end was very efficient. She had told Phil about a lead that came in from the Las Vegas Police Department, and about a subject in a hospital there who was not completely identified but had given the name of Mike Conners. Phil realized that Conners was a very common name, and even though the initial description of the man was similar to his Mike Conners, he knew that it was foolish to get excited too early, and until he had something more definite, he would never be able to get Melissa Conners' hopes up.

After Phil hung up, he continued driving towards his office. He needed to pick up a file and discuss Melissa Conners' request to get away. His superiors would not be happy.

Chapter 3

Sgt. Raymond Tulley of the Las Vegas Metro Police Department stretched out his hand to greet Agent Grant. The two men momentarily sized each other up. Both men were in their thirties. Agent Grant seemed younger, having a fairer complexion. Raymond Tulley was a native of Las Vegas. He was slightly stockier and his skin darker and rougher. One could clearly see that Tulley was more of the rugged outdoor type. Agent Grant sensed that this was a no-nonsense individual that had a slight disliking for law enforcement people of the Federal variety. After they exchanged pleasantries, Sgt. Tulley filled him in.

"Your office called and said to be expecting you. They requested that I place a few men at the hospital to keep a watch over the subject."

"Have you been able to question Mr. Conners yet?" Agent Grant asked.

"No, they have him in some kind of quarantine. He's visible through a two-way mirror only. The hospital said he should be out in about twenty-four hours."

Sgt. Tulley raised his voice slightly. "I still don't understand why the FBI is so interested in this particular person, Mr. Grant, or why the necessity of men to guard him. It would have been nice to know if we were watching over some kind of terrorist or something."

Phil Grant nodded his head, his lips squeezed together as he sensed the irritation in the statement and prepared to answer Sgt. Tulley's question. Placing emphasis on the titles, he said, "First of all, Sergeant, it's Agent Grant. And secondly, if there was some kind of danger to your men, you would have been notified of that fact. I thought my office told you that the men were needed strictly for the subject's protection."

"No, Agent, we weren't told anything of the sort."

"Well, then I apologize if your help has caused your department any inconvenience, and I'll be sure to mention that fact to my superiors in my report."

Sgt. Tulley stopped himself from going further and changed direction.

"Okay, I guess I just don't like being kept in the dark. I have to look out for my own, you know."

"Yes, I understand."

Sgt. Tulley leaned back in his chair, his head just barely touching the wall behind him, and continued his previous line of questioning.

"So, can I assume this subject, who claims to be a Mike Conners, is a misguided witness in your protection program?"

Phil Grant chuckled slightly.

"I'm not at liberty to say yet, and—"

"You wouldn't tell me if he was," Sgt. Tulley interrupted.

"Okay, look, we seem to have gotten off on the on the wrong foot here, Sgt. Tulley, and before we have a complete breakdown of trust and communication, allow me to clear a few things up."

Sgt. Tulley raised his hand in front of Phil Grant's face like a traffic cop trying to signal a large truck to stop at an intersection.

"Wait a minute, Agent Grant, just wait a damn minute. Before you go into some bureaucratic bullshit speech about how we should have cooperation and trust between our departments, let me let you know my take on this." Sgt. Tulley lowered his hands and placed both of them on the edge of his desk and pushed his chair back as if to get up. Instead he placed his hands on his thighs before continuing.

"You don't think much of the local police here or anywhere else. You probably went to college and became an agent right out of your last year. You were probably indoctrinated into the Bureau and fed all sorts of bullshit about how the FBI is the elite law enforcement agency in the country, or maybe even the world, and because of that, you look down on all of us who work the trenches."

Phil Grant couldn't believe what he was hearing and found himself twisting slightly in his chair to make himself more comfortable while Sgt. Tulley continued.

"You think our work is not as important as yours and so you like to keep us in the dark and hope that we'll just accept the little tidbits of information that you feed us, not wanting to ruffle the feathers of the mighty FBI. Well, I don't subscribe to that logic at all. And if you truly want my assistance, you'll admit your shortcomings and tell me what is going on, as I would resent anything else as an insult to my intelligence."

Agent Grant sat staring straight through Sgt. Tulley to the window behind him. He didn't move until he felt he wouldn't be interrupted. His words came slowly and deliberately, as if he were testing Sgt. Tulley's understanding of them.

"Okay, look, I apologize for any misconception you might have gotten from this. And you should know that your opinion of me is probably at least fifty percent correct, but that doesn't change what I need to do to carry out my assignment."

"There was a subject known as Mike Conners, who was in the program, but has mysteriously disappeared. I was the agent in charge of his safety. And I am responsible for him until he either leaves the program, dies, or I get reassigned."

Sgt. Tulley's eyebrows suddenly raised and Agent Grant saw that he softened the officer's opinion of him ever so slightly by this show of confidence in the matter.

"I have to follow up on all leads we receive, and quite frankly, this is the first real one I've gotten."

"Well, OK for now, Agent Grant. Do you have a picture of Mr. Conners on you?"

Agents Grant took the latest one out of his attaché case and placed it on the desk in front Sgt. Tulley.

"From what I've been able to see of the subject, there is a good resemblance. When do you plan on seeing for yourself?"

"Well, twenty-four hours would mean I could interview him by six tonight, but first I think I'll speak with the doctors at the hospital and check on the recovery team."

"Recovery team?" Sgt. Tulley asked.

"Yes, it's a group of agents used any time a subject in the program, who is missing, is located. I put them on stand-by just in case."

Sgt. Tulley's look on his face appeared to Agent Grant as if he should continue to explain, but an intervening police captain who walked into the conversation cut him off.

"Agent Grant, hi, my name is Captain Forrester. I'm in charge of this place while my chief is on vacation." The captain stretched out his arm as Phil Grant rose up to greet him and the two men shook hands.

"I hope the good sergeant has given you what you need so far."

Sgt. Tulley shot a look at Agent Grant and waited for the complaints to flow.

"Sgt. Tulley has been a great help so far, very professional."

"Good," the captain replied. "If there's anything else you need don't hesitate to ask."

"I won't, thanks."

"I'd stay and talk but I have a meeting with the governor which I'm late for already."

The captain looked at Sgt. Tulley one more time before leaving.

"See you tomorrow, Sergeant."

"Yes, sir. Goodbye, Cap."

"That's my cue to be leaving also, Sergeant. I'd like to see the doctors before dinner."

The two men stood before each other and shook hands. Agent Grant could tell by the look on Sgt. Tulley's face that he was grateful for not mentioning their differences to his captain.

"Okay then," Sgt. Tulley said. "Just let me know when my men are no longer needed at the hospital."

"I will."

The drive to the hospital took about ten minutes. And it took another ten minutes for Agent Grant to find his way to the administrative offices of Dr. Trumbull. The men sat across from each other at a dark oak table used for consultation and planning. Ted was seated to the right of Dr. Trumbull.

Dr. Trumbull did most of the talking and within five minutes Phil Grant knew almost as much as the two doctors did in reference to Mike Conners. The only piece of information the doctors kept from him was their experiences that they both had with him. Phil Grant explained to them the Bureau's interest in their patient and the importance of finding out his identity.

"Well, there you have it, Agent Grant, I hope it helps," Alex Trumbull said as he turned to Ted Richards. "Do you have anything for Mr. Grant, Ted?"

"No, I think that's it."

"Thanks for your help, Doctors. I was wondering, did Mr. Conners give out or mention any other names?"

"No, no other names. I was there when he came in, and like I said, at times he was semi-conscious, but I think I would have remembered if he did," Ted said.

"Good, now when do you think I could see him?"

"As soon as he wakes up and I have a chance to examine him. As you know he is in isolation but that shouldn't be a problem," Al said.

"Okay, when that time comes I think it might be best if one of you introduce me as a member of the staff. I don't want to upset Mr. Conners any more than I have to."

The two doctors nodded their approval and stood up. Agent Grant picked up copies of the reports from the table and advised the doctors where he could be located when the time came. He left them in the room and he decided he would try the food at the cafeteria, instead of a local dinner.

Mike Conners sat up in bed and attempted to rub his face with his bandaged hands. The dressing on them was actually a type of glove used for burn victims. His hospital gown was damp from perspiration. His nurse looked up from the chart at the foot of his bed and smiled.

"Well, hello there. It's about time you woke up. We were starting to think you would sleep straight through to winter."

Mike looked at her and spoke.

"Where am I?"

His throat convulsed under the strain, and a coughing fit had the nurse come to his side with a glass of water.

"Whoa, easy there, partner. Here, drink some of this."

Mike gingerly held the glass in his hands as his nurse placed her hand on his back to steady him.

"Small sips till your throat gets used to fluids again. You've been dry for some time"

Mike again tried to speak. "Where am I?" The words flowed a little easier and the nurse backed up as she spoke.

"You're in the special care unit of Las Vegas General Hospital. I'll notify the doctor that you're awake."

Mike again shifted, a worried look on his face, his eyes followed from his glove-covered hands to the contacts attached to his body leading to the equipment surrounding his bed.

"What is all this stuff?"

"Don't worry, It's all for your benefit. We had to keep a close eye on you. The doctor will probably remove it in a little while. Try not to touch your hands."

With that the nurse left. Mike continued to scan the room. There were three sets of equipment surrounding him that looked like small televisions with blips and lines moving across the screens. The room itself was rather large, but his was the only bed in it. A closet with no door was off to his left. The doorway was directly across and about twenty feet from the foot of his bed. To the right of the door was a large mirror, and to Mike's right, about fifteen feet away was another doorway which led to a bathroom. The toilet bowl was visible through it. Two vinyl-covered chairs were arranged facing his bed between him and the doorway. The sight of the commode reminded him that he had the urge to go. That was when he realized that there was a tube inserted in him for that purpose. He began to feel very uncomfortable and shifted and sat upright once again. He turned to look further around and noticed that his bed was against a wall. He also noticed that there were no windows. Looking back toward the mirror he found himself staring at it. There was something unusual about it as it appeared slightly off color. He could not see his reflection in it as it was too far to his right.

He noticed a wire suspended from his bed rail with a button attached to it. He was about to press it when Dr. Trumbull walked through the door.

"Hello there, the ward nurse told me you were awake. My name is Dr. Trumbull." He moved closer but did not extent his hand, and observed for a reaction.

"Hi," Mike said. "How did I get here?"

"A truck driver brought you in to us. Do you remember what happened?"

Mike's brow wrinkled as he tried to piece together his memory.

"I don't remember much of anything. I was driving in a car and it started to rain. I think there were these bright lights ahead of me, and I'm not sure what it was but I remember pulling off the road to avoid them. I don't know, it's all so fuzzy, like trying to recall a dream."

Dr. Trumbull looked at his patient and then picked up one of the chairs and turned it around to use its back as a rest for his arms. A low-throated hum emerged from his throat, the kind that tells you more questions were coming.

"When you were admitted, you were in a semi-conscious state. You gave us a name of Mike Conners. Is that correct?"

"Yes, that's my name." A strange look came over him, and he looked away toward the wall. He seemed more confused and said again, "Yes that's it, but why can't I remember anything else about myself. I mean when you ask me, I feel confident about saying my name, but I can't tell you more about myself. I should know myself, where I live, or how I got to this spot." An empty panic took hold, like being lost in the woods. Mike looked back at the doctor, who tried to console his patient.

"Now just relax. Don't panic. Together I'm sure we will figure this out. You've been through quite an ordeal and it will take some time for your mind to sort it all out."

Phil Grant stared at the patient from behind the two-way mirror. He thought that it looked like Mike Conners but he seemed slightly thinner from when he last saw him. His voice was raspier, but that could just be the result of his ordeal in the desert. He listened intently to Dr. Trumbull's interview and wondered about his mentioning that the last thing he remembered was driving in the rain, as it hadn't rained in about a month. He tried to pick out something that would confirm his suspicions of doubt in regards to his true identity. The agent waited anxiously for his turn to speak with him. He had decided that he would be introduced as a psychiatrist specializing in memory retention. He wondered if he would recognize him. If he did, then it would be somewhat of a relief. He still felt guilty in regards to Mike Conners' disappearance and wanted to right the situation and reunite him with his family. He knew he must be careful though, for if this was some kind of imposter, he would open up the rest of the Conners family to danger.

Some ten minutes went by before Dr. Trumbull finished and retreated to the room where Agent Grant awaited.

"Well, he's expecting you. Just try to go easy, he's experiencing some frustration and confusion due to his lapse of memory."

"I'll do my best, Doc."

Agent Grant took a deep breath and entered Mike's room.

"Hello, Mr. Conners, I'm Dr. Casey. I specialize in physiological disorders and memory loss."

"I know, I know, Dr. Trumbull just told me you'd be in."

Agent Grant adjusted the chair and sat down to be close

enough to get a good read on Mike's facial expressions but not too close as to make him uncomfortable.

"I see by your chart that you've been through quite a bad time being lost in the desert. You're very fortunate someone found you."

"Yes I know," Mike said as he shifted in his bed.

"I've been observing your conversation with Dr. Trumbull from the next room." Agent Grant motioned to the large mirror on the far wall.

"I thought so. I mean it caught my eye ever since I woke up, and I just had this feeling of being watched."

"That's good, Mr. Conners, that shows that you perceive your surroundings, and observing in that way is related to cognitive reasoning, which of course is related to memory and recall on a basic level."

Agent Grant knew he must be careful here in his effort to sound like he was an expert and gain the trust of Mike Conners. He knew he now must proceed with his interview and at the same time try to stay away from actually trying to help him.

"Woo, don't confuse me."

"All I mean to say is that I don't think your memory problems will last long." Agent Grant hesitated momentarily and then continued. "I know you haven't been awake long, but can you recall any thoughts or maybe dreams you might have had, anything that seems familiar?"

Mike Conners looked up at the ceiling and then down at his blanket.

"No, not really. I mean, I get this feeling of loneliness that I miss or I'm supposed to be with someone, I think, I'm just not sure."

"Well, it's something that we can work on, Mr. Conners," the agent said.

Mike Conners suddenly shot a look at Agent Grant as if he was just slapped in the face. The agent noticed this and asked, "What is it, Mr. Conners?"

Mike's brow wrinkled. "I'm not sure, but when you just said my name, your voice sounded familiar to me, like I've heard you say it before."

"Possibly another association you're having with someone else from your past, as I'm sure we've never met."

Phil Grant found himself becoming uneasy and decided to end the interview.

"We'll talk some more soon. I want to go over some of your tests Dr. Trumbull took."

He got up from the chair and started to leave.

"When will you be back?"

"Probably tomorrow. Get some rest."

Agent Grant thought that the resemblance and mannerism was very close to what he remembered of Mike, but there was still enough doubt for him to keep his guard up. He knew he needed to wait for Mike's hands to heal enough for fingerprints to be taken. He went to look for Dr. Trumbull.

Dr. Trumbull and Alex were standing by the nurses' station when Agent Grant found them.

"Well, what do you think?" Alex said to Phil as he placed a pen in his top pocket.

"I'm not sure. The resemblance is uncanny but I can't get enough information to make any judgments. How much longer till we can take his fingerprints?"

"The nurse is scheduled to change his dressing after dinner. I'll be there to examine him and should be able to get a better idea then."

"Good," Agent Grant said. "You have my cell phone number and here is my pager number." He gave a business card to both doctors. "If I don't hear from you by tonight, then I'll call back tomorrow. I'm also having one of my agents take over for the local police. I think it would appear less menacing to Mr. Conners anyway if he happens to see someone standing by his door not wearing a uniform and gun. I don't want him to think he is under any kind of suspicion."

Ted Richards told the nurse on station to disconnect Mike from the equipment and get him something to eat. He then left with Al to have dinner at a local restaurant.

Chapter 4

At seven-thirty in the evening when Dr. Richards came into Mike's room, he was surprised to see Mike walking out of the bathroom. He stopped a few feet from the door.

"How you feeling, Mr. Conners?"

"Much better, thank you. It was a little difficult to use the bathroom with these gloves on, but I managed." Mike sat on his bed and continued. "My hands don't hurt at all. Look I can even make a fist."

The doctor took Mike's right hand and examined it by applying slight pressure in different spots.

"Does this bother you?"

"No, not at all."

The doctor proceeded to use the same technique on the left hand with the same result.

"Hmm, well let's take the dressing off and see what it looks like."

Ted called in the staff nurse to assist him and had her bring in some new dressing. She stood next to him and held Mike's arm as the doctor cut the glove bandage off. He was just making his last cut and then the glove fell to the floor. As he turned Mike's hand over to examine it, he heard the nurse give out a short gasp. The nurse looked at the doctor, the doctor looked at the nurse and then at Mike and back to his hand.

"What is it? What's wrong?" Mike said, as he looked for himself and turned his hand over and back again.

"This is incredible. I've never seen a person with the type of burns you had heal so fast," Ted said as he continued to examine Mike's hand. Mike pulled away from the doctor and stared at it himself, closing and opening it several times.

"I don't know what to say, Doc. I never really saw my hands before they were bandaged, and I can't recall if they were injured anyway. So it doesn't surprise me."

Ted removed the glove from the other hand in the same manner and found the same result. Both hands appeared completely healed.

"Well, what do you think, Doc? Maybe my hands weren't as badly burned as you thought?"

Ted could only shake his head and let out a short grunt. He was happy for his patient, and he didn't feel it would do him any good to emphasize to him the extent to which his hands were burned. Taking into account the events of the previous evening with him and Doctor Trumbull, he thought it best to let it go for now.

"I guess you were in better shape than I thought, Mr. Conners."

The staff nurse was still shaking her head, which caught Ted's eye. In a somewhat stern voice and waving his hand towards the door he said, "Nurse, will you find Dr. Trumbull for me, now."

She hesitated momentarily and with a blank stare looked at Mike Conners.

"Nurse Anderson!"

Ted's second request snapped her out of her stupor.

"Yes, Doctor, right away," she said as she did an about-face and left hurriedly.

Chapter 5

Phil Grant sat at the booth farthest from the door. His coffee was cold from sitting too long and the cheesecake smelled to him as if it had stayed in the refrigerator too long and absorbed the odor from the next closest food. He couldn't tell what it was and decided to let it sit. The restaurant was crowded and most of the people looked agitated as there wasn't enough staff to accommodate them. The waitress glanced his way and smiled. It was not a full smile and started out more as a smirk as she finished picking up a tip from the most recently used table. Phil could sense her disappointment as she stuffed the bills into her uniform. Her gaze lingered long enough to take her to where he sat.

"Hi, this table is not normally in my section, but I noticed you looked like you wanted something and I believe your waitress went on a break, so can I get you more coffee?"

"Yes, please."

"Oh, I see you didn't care for the cheesecake. Is there something else I can bring you, something a little fresher perhaps."

"What do you suggest?" Phil asked as he pushed the plate to the edge of the table.

"Well, the strawberry shortcake would be my choice as I know it just arrived an hour ago. And I won't even charge you extra."

"Sounds good to me."

"Good, I'll be right back," she said as she cleared his table and walked away. He noticed she didn't really walk, she sort of glided, and right before she disappeared through the kitchen doors, she took one more look in his direction. He couldn't tell if she was attracted to him or just being nice to try for a bigger tip. He thought about it for a minute and decided he was much too skeptical for it to be anything else but her hoping for more money. A minute later the waitress returned with Phil's request. As she set it down, he found himself smiling as he looked into her eyes.

"Thank you."

"You're welcome," she said, and then moved on to another part of the room. As she stood at another table, Phil could not help but notice that she positioned herself facing his table and would glance his way from time to time as she took the customer's order. With each look, he found himself again smiling. Some ten minutes passed before he realized the attraction was more than he was used to. He found himself becoming uncomfortable with it and didn't know why. *Damn, I've been alone too long,* he thought. His thoughts were interrupted by the vibrations of his cell phone. He didn't like leaving the ringer on in public places as he didn't like to bring attention to himself.

"Yeah," he spoke into it as he turned his back to the room.

"Phil, this is Robert Durham."

"Rob, how the hell are you?"

"Normally I'd be great, but it seems we have a slight problem with one of our guests."

"Which one?" Phil said as he turned to once again face the room of people.

"Melissa Conners."

The silence from Agent Grant's end was a little bit longer than Robert Durham could take.

"Phil, you still there?"

"Uh, yeah, I was just thinking."

Phil Grant found himself staring again at the waitress and had to look away to maintain his attention to the phone call.

"So, what's the problem?"

"I believe she checked out."

"What?" Suddenly Phil sat up.

"I was making the scheduled phone check of the residence but didn't get a response. I attempted a few more, and when that failed, I decided to try the alarm system to see if I could hear anything in the house. When I didn't detect anything, I decided to pay her a visit. The place is empty and the car is gone."

"What do you mean empty? Like furniture and everything."

"No, I meant she took a lot of her clothes."

"Terrific," Phil said. "Just what I need, a careless female exposing herself to bigger problems than she can handle."

"The office wants you to see if you can locate her."

Phil sighed. "Do they know I'm supposed to be checking out this other identity thing here. I mean, this could be the missing piece to the puzzle."

"Of course, I understand. It's just that she is your responsibility also."

"Alright, I'm kind of at a standstill here until I can get some prints. The last I heard it could be a few days. I'll be there as soon as I can."

Agent Grant quickly dialed the hospital. The receptionist was unable to locate Dr. Trumbull, so he left a voice message explaining that he would be back in a day or so. He spoke with the agent assigned to Mike's room and advised him of his need to leave for a bit, and to make the necessary arrangements for coverage.

Chapter 6

Dr. Alex Trumbull looked at Mike Conners' hands and asked him how he felt. Mike smiled and said, "I feel fine. I mean, except for not knowing who I am or where I live or other things most people remember."

Al turned to Dr. Richards and said, "Well, what do you think?"

"I don't know what to think. I mean it's incredible. You're a very lucky guy, Mr. Conners, with great recuperative abilities."

"Thanks but I still wish my memory would catch up to the rest of all this good fortune you're talking about."

Dr. Trumbull smiled and said, "Don't worry, we'll work on it. Meanwhile I think I'll have you moved to another room."

"Thanks," Mike said. "I hope something with a window. And do you think I could get some clothes?" Ted looked at Dr. Trumbull and motioned him to step outside.

Al looked at Mike and said, "I'll see what I can do."

The two doctors stepped out into the hall and moved away from where the FBI agent was posted.

"What are you doing Al?" Ted asked.

"What do you mean?"

"We don't know who this guy is for sure, and neither does the

FBI. And have you forgotten what happened to us the other morning?"

"No, I haven't forgotten any of that. I just think it would help his mental recovery if we moved him to a better atmosphere, one that doesn't make him feel like a lab rat."

"And what do we tell the FBI?"

Al shot a glance at the agent watching Mike's room.

"We'll just tell them the patient has improved to a point that staying in isolation might be counterproductive. Anyway we need that room for other patients."

Ted slowly shook his head. "I don't know about this."

Al placed his hand on Ted's shoulder. "Don't worry, I'll make arrangements to move Mike to the suites we use for the dignitaries that we get from out of town. They're still out of the way from the other population and I don't think even if Mr. Conners was a mass murderer, he could jump from the seventh floor to escape."

"Okay, then you're the boss. I just hope I don't have to say I told you so if things go sour."

"Good, I'll contact the ward nurse for that floor and you see about getting him some clothes. Also, let's set something up with a real psychiatrist to help him with his memory."

Ted nodded his head in the direction of the agent. "What about him?"

"Don't worry I'll take care of it. Agent Grant left me a voicemail telling me he would be back in a day or so. I don't think this agent is allowed to make any decisions on his own, so I don't think he'll give us a problem with the move."

The next morning Mike Conners accompanied with Dr. Trumbull walked through the door of his new room. It was more like a hotel room than a hospital room. The color scheme was tan and golden brown. The room even had a separate couch for guests and its own little refrigerator. The view from the seventh floor was of the strip, downtown. The Luxor Hotel with its pyramid shape and the MGM Grand Hotel with its Lions were magnificent to Mike.

"This is much nicer, Doc. And look at this view."

"I'm glad you like it," Al said as he placed Mike's chart in the pocket behind the door.

"I managed to get you a set of clothes. They're hanging in the closet. I guessed on the size so don't be upset if the fit is off a little."

"Thanks," Mike said. He walked over to the closet and peered in. "I just thought of something, Doc."

"You mean you remember something?"

"No, but the thought just occurred to me." Mike hesitated as he looked around. "How is all of this going too paid for?"

"Don't worry, you forget this is a city-run hospital and Las Vegas is one of the richest cities in the world. I'm sure we can afford it for you. Anyway I don't see you staying here all that long. Just make yourself comfortable."

Al walked out of the room and down the hall to the waiting agent who was sitting on a couch with a clear view of the doorway to Mike's room. It was an ideal spot to be stationed as the room was at the end of a hall and there was no way out except to go past the agent. Even with Mike's door open, he could not see the agent unless he stepped out into the hall. It also gave the hospital staff more privacy in treating Mike.

"I see you found the best seat in the house," Al said as he approached the agent. "Did you get to speak to Mr. Grant about the change in rooms for Mr. Conners?"

"No, I've been trying to reach him but I can't get through to his cell phone."

"That's probably because your trying from your cell phone. Anyway the hospital has strict rules about using cell phones in the building," Al said as he pointed toward a large white sign with red letters stating so. "There are a number of instruments that it could interfere with. Just go over to that desk and ask to use that phone."

"Okay, thanks, I didn't mean to break the rules and I hope I didn't screw up any equipment for you."

"I'm not worried about the equipment, just the patients that might be attached to them."

"Oh, yeah, I didn't even think about that. Sorry," the agent said as his face clearly turned a shade of red from his embarrassment.

Al shook his head and walked over to the nurses' station.

The stern-looking nurse behind the desk had a phone in one hand and a pen in the other.

She glanced up to see Dr. Trumbull leaning on the counter awaiting her to acknowledge him. She stopped talking long enough to hear his instruction.

"This is Agent—what did you say your name was?" He turned to look him in the face.

"Martin, Tom Martin."

"Yes that's it,. Agent Martin, this is Nurse Belsong. Nurse Belsong, any time Mr. Martin needs the phone, let him use it."

Nurse Belsong did not answer but shook her head in agreement and went right back to her writing. Al smiled at the agent and walked away.

It did not take long for Mike Conners to get used to his new surroundings. The clothes supplied to him were a good fit and he looked at himself in the mirror with satisfaction. He went to the window and looked down at the city below. From his perch he could not make out faces and thought that they were all just like him. From here they were just people without any identities. He didn't know them, but they knew themselves. They knew who they were, where they were going and where they had been. He didn't have that luxury and for an instant a mild panic crept over him. He quickly dismissed the thought and returned to the mirror. He stepped close and examined his features. Opening his mouth as wide as he could, looking inside, he bared his teeth as a chimpanzee might do looking at visitors in a zoo. He found himself making distorted faces and then relaxing to stare some more at the stranger staring back. *Who the hell are you?* he thought. When no answer came to him, he felt his frustration level rising. He turned and walked to the bed, sat down and noticed a menu for food sitting on the chair next to him. He picked it up and started going over all the options. For breakfast he could have eggs made any number of ways, or French toast or waffles. As he mulled this over, the door to his room opened and a young nurse walked through the door.

"Hello, Mr. Conners, my name is Nurse Farley. Dr. Richards sent me here to give you these newspapers to read. He thought maybe it would help trigger something in your memory."

Nurse Farley was in her late twenties. She was very attractive, petite with golden blonde hair and the clearest blue eyes. The kind that could look right into one's soul. She stood in front of Mike and stretched out her arms to give them over. Mike sat there staring at her and didn't say a word. She smiled and said, "Mr. Conners." He jerked free of his stupor and apologized for staring.

"I'm sorry, Mrs.—what did you say your name was?"

"It's Nurse Farley, and it's alright. I get that a lot from men the first time we meet."

They both chuckled and Mike felt relieved that she was professional enough to say something to break the awkward moment.

"Good idea, thanks." He placed the bundle at the foot of his bed and quickly turned to pick back up the menu as he asked, "What time is it.? I noticed there isn't a clock in here but I'm getting hungry."

"That was going to be my next question, and it's 8:20. What would you like to eat?"

Without looking up Mike blurted out, "I think I'll have the French toast. I like the way your mom makes them."

"Excuse me," the nurse said.

"I mean, I don't know why I said that. It sort of just came out."

The two of them looked at each other, another awkward moment passed before the door to Mike's room opened and Dr. Trumbull entered.

"Well, I see you got the papers Dr. Richards sent over. Sometimes reading helps trigger people's memories. You never know, right."

Mike and Nurse Farley looked at Dr. Trumbull, agreeing with his statement.

Dr. Trumbull continued. "I've set you up with an excellent doctor to help you with your memory. His name is Dr. Harold Trent. Your first consultation will be tomorrow at 11 a.m."

"What happened to Dr. Casey?"

"He had to be reassigned, but he conferred with Dr. Trent before he left. They are both excellent; I just feel Dr. Trent has more experience than Dr. Casey." Dr. Trumbull could not help but feel a twinge of guilt as he told this lie, but knowing it was for his own good, quickly dismissed his feelings.

Mike shrugged his shoulders, picked up a copy of the *Los Angeles Times* and looked at Nurse Farley. "Will you be gone long?"

The nurse smiled and said, "Why, do you want to read a little before you eat?"

"No, actually, I figured I'd read later."

"Okay then, I'll be right back."

She left the room and Mike returned his attention to Dr. Trumbull.

"I'm glad she left, Doc. She makes me nervous for some reason. Anyway I said something really stupid to her before you got here." Mike explained what he said to her and thought that she reminded him of someone, but he couldn't remember who.

The doctor picked up Mike's chart from the end of the bed and wrote down some notes. Placing the clipboard back on its hook he looked back at Mike and said, "Don't worry about it. I imagine you're going to be saying more things like that before your memory returns. I'll check in on you later in the day and in the morning before Dr. Trent gets here."

Dr. Trumbull left and Mike moved the papers to a small table in the corner of the room. It had a high back chair with a comfortable cushion. After turning on the light above it, Mike began sorting the papers. The doctor had supplied him with a good variety of reading material. There was the *New York Times*, *The San Francisco Examiner* and the *Wall Street Journal*. A paper called the Star and one called the *Enquirer*. He placed them in an order and started with the *Times*. The headlines referred to the President's speech on the economy, and another described the systematic break-up of another internet company. He skimmed through both quickly not giving them much thought as he didn't feel it affected him. He then began to think of how much of what is printed would affect him, a person with no identity, and seemingly no connections. A slight depression rolled over him like a fog from the sea. He could feel that panicky, lost feeling he had felt before returning. The door to his room opened and Nurse Farley entered, announcing that breakfast had arrived. The fog lifted and Mike, seeing her smile, felt the warmth of the moment.

"What are you reading?" she asked.

"Headlines of break-ups and economy woes." Mike forced a smile and stood up to approach the food cart.

"Would you like to eat at that table?"

"Sure, why not," Mike said and sat back down. Nurse Farley moved the stack of newspapers to a small couch on a far wall and placed the breakfast in front of Mike. As she did the smell of the food caused Mike to breathe in through his nose and comment on it.

"Smells good," he said.

She managed a small laugh barely audible but enough to make him comment. "You know something about my breakfast you're not commenting on, or do you think I don't know any better, and you're waiting for me to taste it."

She did not look up but continued to arrange the remainder of his food on the table.

"No, It's perfectly good food, it's just that it's hospital food, the same as we serve to all the patients. Nothing to get excited about." She finally looked him in the face and said, "I guess if I went through what you've been through then it would smell delicious to me also."

Mike heard what she said and found himself staring intently at her. He was thinking and trying to figure out why she felt familiar to him. Nurse Farley felt his glare and found herself staring back. Another awkward moment passed and then she said, "Who do you think I look like?"

"I'm not sure. What makes you think you look familiar to me?"

"You just said that I look familiar to you."

"No, I didn't say anything."

"Yes you did. I heard you. You said, 'You look familiar to me.'"

"I never said anything. I never opened my mouth. What, you read minds, too?"

"Okay forget it." She finished arranging his food and started to leave. "I'll be back in about an hour to take your pressure and give you something to help you relax if you want."

"Thanks, Nurse, I hope I didn't offend you or anything."

"No, way." The nurse left the room. As soon as she was in the hall she started to think about what just happened. It suddenly occurred to her that when she was looking at Mike, she heard him as plain as day, but she couldn't recall if his mouth was open or his lips were moving. A wave of goose bumps suddenly came over her. She shook off the feeling and went about her duties.

Chapter 7

Agent Grant sat outside Melissa Conners' residence staring at the house for some ten minutes as he awaited Agent Durham's arrival. It was another beautiful day in the neighborhood; he remembered that the last time he was here the weather was also nice. He again thought of how nice it would be to live here and found himself daydreaming of a life he hoped someday he could have. This time he was in a painting van. His outfit naturally matched his profession. Agent Durham's van showed up and pulled into the driveway, and Phil put his dream on hold. Both men got out and approached the front door. Robert Durham was the younger of the two. He was in his mid-twenties with brown hair and a stocky build. His painter's uniform consisted of trousers with large pockets and gray work shirt. It seemed a little tight and uncomfortable. The large pockets were perfect though for his duty weapon and as his left hand pushed the door open, his right was firmly holding his service weapon, a glock semi auto. He went in first while Phil waited momentarily on the front stoop. This was more of a precautionary measure than anything else. He signaled for Phil to enter and both of them systematically started a routine search of the premises. Both did not speak until they were satisfied that they were alone.

As they met in the living room Phil said, "Well, I guess you were right. She's gone. Let's see if we can find anything here to tell us where she went." The two agents examined the house more closely. When Phil got to the trash can by a desk in the living room he picked it up and emptied its contents onto the desk top.

"Oh, sure. let's make as much a mess as we can," Agent Durham said as he opened the desk drawers. "You know how much of a clean freak Melissa could be. She is surely not going to appreciate that."

"Shut up, Bob. By the time we leave she'll never know we were here."

In looking through the contents, Phil noticed a crumpled piece of paper, which came from a pad that was next to the phone. He laid it flat on the desk. "It looks like she wrote something on this and then scribbled it out. Let's get a copy of the phone numbers called from this phone to see what comes up."

Phil used his cell to call into his office to have them run a check on the phone. While they waited for the results, the two agents continued to look around.

"Judging by the amount of clothes missing, I'd say she was planning on being gone for a while," Agent Durham said.

"I don't know." Phil added. "She liked a lot of clothes anyway. I remember when she first came into the program. In that first weekend she tried taking four suitcases with her. When I told her she could only bring one at the moment and that we would sent for more clothes later she kind of freaked."

Agent Durham grunted. "By the way I haven't tried to contact her parents yet to see if they heard from her."

"Good," Phil said as he sat on the desk next to the phone awaiting a reply from his office. "I don't relish the thought of dealing with them just yet. Melissa's father can be a real pain in the ass. He tried running all kinds of interference when she told him her decision to enter the program with Mike."

Another grunt from Agent Durham, who added, "Wealthy people will do that; it's like they always gotta be in control."

"Yeah, he wanted to whisk her away to some foreign country. He thinks he can give her better protection than we could, and if something does happen to her, he'll probably try suing us."

"What's this 'us' bit? You mean you."

"I mean 'us,' as in the FBI."

"Oh, yeah right," Agent Durham said.

Mike's cell beeped and he put it to his ear, "Yeah." A slight pause and then another "yeah." As he listened, he began to fumble for a pen in his pocket and started to write. "Wait a second, I can't write that fast. Okay, go ahead. Yeah, terrific, well how's that for a coincidence. When? Okay, good. Thanks. We'll check it out." Phil disconnected and reread what was on the paper. "Okay, you'll never guess where Melissa made several calls to."

Agent Durham wrinkled his brow and turned up both hands. "Hell I don't know. Her parents' house. Oh, wait a minute, I heard you say coincidence." He stared a moment at the piece of paper in Phil's hands and then said. "Las Vegas!"

"Bingo, give the man a prize," Agent Grant said as he stuffed the paper in his pocket.

"Actually it makes perfect sense. The last time I spoke to her, she was complaining about wanting to get away as she was bored and tired of being by herself. I know she likes to gamble, so there you go. I just find it weird that there's a guy in a hospital in the same city that could very well be her husband, and she doesn't even know it. The trace report from the office listed three hotels that she made calls to. The MGM Grand, the Excalibur, and the Luxor."

Robert Durham smiled slightly and added, "Well, at least the three are fairly close to each other. Do you want a locate team to try and pick her up?"

"No, we can handle it ourselves. Anyway I don't want to spook her as she kind of has to be handled gently."

"Worried about her father again, are we?"

Phil Grant just shook his head and grunted, "No, not really."

"In fact, if we find her fast enough, I won't have to speak to the pain-in-the-ass at all."

Phil cleaned up the mess he made on the desk top, and both agents did a walk-through of the residence again to make sure it looked as it did before they arrived. As they approached the front door to leave, Bob Durham said, "I just have to stop and pick up some clothes and then I'll meet you at the airport in about an hour."

"Sounds good. I'll be by the American Airlines desk waiting," Phil added.

As he walked to his van, Phil Grant dialed the cell phone of the agent he left at the hospital. An annoying message kept repeating the phrase, "I'm sorry, we are unable to complete your call, and you are being transferred to a message mail box."

Damn cell phones never work when you want them to, he thought.

Then it occurred to him that it was because of the hospital that he couldn't get through, and he remembered the restrictions they had against using them anyway. He dialed the hospital directly got the main switchboard and asked for Dr. Trumbull. The receptionist kept him waiting for about two minutes before she returned. "I'm sorry. Dr. Trumbull is in a meeting and asked not to be disturbed."

"Okay great! Then could you connect me to the nurses' station on two south?"

The voice on the other end answered back, "Stand by, please."

Several strange buzzing sounds attacked Agent Grant's ears and then the phone went silent.

"What the hell happened now?" Phil found himself saying out loud. He grunted and put his phone away deciding instead to wait until he got to his hotel room before trying to make contact again. As he drove away, he again looked around the neighborhood and thought of how nice it would be to live here. The lawns were so green and well-kept. The sounds of children playing and neighbors calling to each other to say hello were comforting. He began looking at each house and in his mind he pictured himself living in each one. He decided that a ranch would suit his personality. He didn't have to have a white picket fence or two-car garage, just something to call his own. His thoughts were suddenly interrupted by the sounds of a siren and flashing lights coming from a police car behind him.

He pulled over to let the car pass but it didn't. The police car stopped behind him. Agent Grant could see the officer through his rearview mirror. He noticed that the officer was alone, but that could change at any moment. Just as he finished thinking this, a second patrol unit pulled up from the other direction and parked across the street. Phil watched the second police officer exit his vehicle and move to the passenger side and stand there, positioning his unit between himself and the roadway. Agent Grant felt this was a little unusual. He looked for the first officer, but he did not see anyone in the rearview mirror. He found himself feeling uneasy about this and started to look over his left shoulder. Just as he did, he was startled from a tapping sound coming from his passenger side window. He could see the officer from the waist up and was somewhat surprised to see she was female. She was wearing dark colored sunglasses and was making a circular gesture with her hands. Agent Grant took this to mean that she wanted him to roll down his window. He awkwardly reached over to do so and as he did, his driver's door flew open.

"Don't move!" came a male voice from the second officer, who was now standing next to him. Agent Grant could tell by the sound of his voice that failure to comply with this command could result in someone getting hurt.

"I'm a federal agent. My ID is in my left rear pocket," replied Phil.

"I also have a glock service weapon on my right side," he added.

"Back out of your vehicle and keep your hands where I can see them," came the response from the officer.

Agent Grant slid backward out of the vehicle and kept his hands raised above his head. The officer placed his hand on his shoulder and pushed him up against the vehicle. The female officer had moved around to the same side as the male officer.

Agent Grant could feel a hand searching him and removing his weapon and ID.

"Okay, sir, turn around," the female voice said.

Phil did so and lowered his hands, clasping them in front. He was now able to see both officers in front of him. The male was holstering a weapon.

"What's the problem, Officers?" asked Phil

The male officer was looking at Agent Grant's ID and started repeating what he was reading.

"'Field Agent Phillip Grant, Federal Bureau of Investigation Special Operations Section.' Well, that sounds impressive. Do you have a driver's license to go with this and the registration for your vehicle?"

Phil found himself getting annoyed at the tone in the voice of the officer, but decided not to let it bother him.

"Yes, I do, would you like to see them?"

"Yes, I would."

Phil slowly removed his wallet and gave over his license.

"The registration is located in the glove box, I think; it's a fleet vehicle so I can't be sure."

The male officer smirked, took the license and moved back a step to look at it.

"Okay, I'm going to go check this out, Julie," he said and then retreated to his police vehicle.

"Do you have any idea why you were stopped?" asked the female officer.

"No, not at all, what did I do?"

"We've had a number of burglaries in the area, so patrols have been stepped up, and we check out a lot of vehicles that we find passing through. In checking your vehicle, I could not locate any record of it on file. Also I couldn't help but notice that the van is empty. No paints, brushes, ladders or anything else that would help a real painter do his job."

Agent Grant chuckled slightly and responded, "Wow, you're good. It's nice to know that the police department is so efficient."

He could feel her cold stare right through her Vidal Sassoon glasses, which he decided to ignore.

"So, Julie, how long have you been a police officer?"

She ignored his attempt at conversation and said, "That's not the response I'm looking for, sir."

"Oh, I didn't know I was supposed to respond to your statement. I thought you were just looking for approval of your patrol abilities."

She didn't respond to his statement and gave no indication through her body language that this annoyed her and continued on.

"So, Mr. Grant, what are you doing here?"

"You can call me Phil," he said. "After all I know your first name and called you by it. I think it's only fair, don't you?"

Her reply came quicker this time.

"Mr. Grant, I don't know if you're trying to take me off the track or you just like to be disrespectful of authority, but either way, it's not appreciated at the moment."

Agent Grant realized that this was going nowhere and decided to try honesty.

"Alright then, Officer..." he tried reading her name tag and added, "Monroe is it?"

I really can't explain to you why I'm in the area, as to do so might compromise my assignment. All you really need to know is that I'm an FBI agent and I'm working on something."

She again had no reaction to this except for a shifting in her stance.

She was about to say something when the male officer returned.

"Alright, I have enough information for now," he said as he gave back the paperwork to Agent Grant. "It seems you are who you say you are and this vehicle is registered to the federal government so I have no reason to hold you. Anyway if I'm wrong then at least I know where to find you."

Phil smiled a half smirking smile and couldn't resist adding his own punch line.

"Yeah and if you two aren't cops, I'll know where to find you also." The two officers looked at each other with droll and quizzical expressions.

His next comment was stopped before it came out by the raspy sound of the officer's portable radio.

"Headquarters to unit 360."

The female officer had one of those microphones that attach to the applet of the shirt. She reached up and pressed it to reply.

"Three-sixty!"

The voice came back

"We just received an alarm indication from 39 Gardeners Way."

The male officer immediately left as the cop named Julie gave her response.

"Ten-four, units 360 and 362 are responding. We are over one block, and should be there in two minutes."

She was already in motion before she finished her sentence leaving Agent Grant before he could have any more fun with them.

As he turned to get in his vehicle a sickening sinking feeling overtook him as he realized the female officer still had his service weapon.

"Shit, damn, asshole," were all the expletives he could come up with. *I can't believe how stupid I get sometimes, especially around women,* he thought. Phil knew he had no other alternative but to follow them to their assignment and retrieve his gun. As he was starting his van, he saw the patrol units through his rearview mirror make a quick right at the intersection behind him. He thought of the transmission he heard from the police radio and the information relayed by the female officer and hoped that the alarm would be false as he didn't need to complicate his day. He made a right turn and went down one block. The sign for the road read "Turtle Cove Lane." He kept going and when he came to the next intersection he saw the sign read "Allison Way." A frustrated feeling came over him as he wondered where and how much further it would be to Gardeners Way. He couldn't imagine where the two officers disappeared, as they were not that far ahead of him. An instant later, he realized what happened and more thoughtful expletives danced in his head. "Shit, how stupid can I get, I was looking in a rear-view mirror. I bet they made a left instead of a right." The vehicle swerved to the right and then the left as Phil executed a quick U-turn. Four blocks in the other direction, he found Gardeners Way. Both police units were parked in front of 37 Gardeners, a dark colored van was in the driveway with out-of-state plates. Phil knew it was good procedure not to park in front of an alarm location and so parked on the other side of the residence at number 41. The agent got out of his vehicle and looked around. There was no one in front and so he cautiously started to move to the area of the police units to await their return. He knew it would be foolish and even dangerous to enter onto the property. As he stood there, he could see into one of the vehicles. The muffled voice of a dispatcher could be heard from within. There on the floor and between the front split bench seats lay his service weapon. He thought of just retrieving it and going on his way and actually tried the door, but it was locked. He looked toward the house and from this angle he could see a bilco door, which probably led to the basement, was open. A loud delivery truck drove slowly by. Its operator appeared to be trying to read the addresses as he passed. As the truck entered Phil's line of sight, momentarily blocking his view, he heard yelling coming from the direction of the side yard. Two loud pops echoed throughout the neighborhood.

The truck continued down the street and Agent Grant found himself frozen as the new scene appeared before him. A tall, heavyset white male was standing over the female officer, a gun pointing down at her. There was no movement from her and Agent Grant feared the worst. He tried to duck down before being noticed, without success. The man began moving in his direction. Phil looked around and realized he was in a bad location. A locked police car and maybe 200 feet were the only protection between himself and certain death. The man was walking at a fast pace, the gun pointed in Phil's direction. The assailant bent down several times trying to see Phil's location from under the police car. Phil shook off the helpless feeling he had and started kicking the driver's side window of the police vehicle. The first attempt caused a sharp pain to grip his ankle as his foot bounced off the window. On the third attempt the glass gave way. The forward movement of the assailant continued to within seventy feet. Phil unlocked the door and dove into the front seat. He reached for his service weapon and just as he did, the passenger side window exploded from a round fired from the weapon of the assailant. The bullet hit the air bag assembly of the steering wheel causing it to activate. Its force momentarily caused Phil to lose his grip on his weapon. The assailant's forward movement now took him to within fifty feet of Agent Grant. Phil raised his gun out the window towards the man as he continued his advance. Phil hoped that the determination of the assailant caused him to continue on the straight course as he visualized it. He fired his weapon seven times before attempting to see where the bullets went.

Cautiously but quickly Phil raised his head as far as permitted to glance in the direction of his attacker. He saw nothing and suddenly feared an attack from the rear. He slithered back out of the patrol vehicle, shards of glass cutting into one of his arms. He found himself sitting on the roadway and glanced around but found no danger. Getting to a crouched position he was able to get a clear view of the scene in front of him. There on the ground about ten feet from the police unit the man lay face down on the lawn. Clearly shaken but highly pissed off at what just occurred, Phil approached his attacker and secured the handgun which was a few feet away. A large exit wound could be seen on the rear of his head and so Phil knew the fight was over. His attention now turned to the officer near the bilco doors. As he ran to her location he fumbled for his cell phone and dialed 911.

"This is Special Agent Phillip Grant of the Federal Bureau of Investigation…" His conversation with the police continued until all the information known was exhausted. He knelt down next to the fallen officer and checked for vital signs. A shaking hand suddenly grabbed Phil by the arm and through pale lips he could hear her.

"Where is he, look out, he has a gun." Phil smiled down at her, thankful she was still alive.

"Don't worry, Officer Monroe, he's dead."

He held her hand and she coughed slightly. Phil could see a slight trickle of blood spill from her mouth. She tried to talk more but her voice was too low for him to make out what she was saying over the arriving police and ambulance units.

"Don't talk, just relax," were the only words that seemed appropriate. He felt her grip go limp as she fell out of consciousness. Within seconds the paramedics were upon them and a police sergeant was getting all the pertinent information he could from Agent Grant. Phil knew this was just the start of what would be a long day for him. He dreaded the forms and the questions that needed answers but knew of their necessity. He knew he could have avoided all of this if he wasn't so careless about his weapon or hadn't engaged the officers in meaningless conversation. But then again he also thought if he wasn't there at all maybe she would be dead.

He followed behind one of the ambulance personnel to the rig; he found himself asking, "What do you think?"

The man stepped back away from the rear of the ambulance, shook his head and said, "It doesn't look to good. One of the bullets found its way under her vest. She has a lot of internal damage."

Phil found himself mouthing the word, "Shit," and looking at the medic he said, "I wish there was something I could have done to prevent this."

The man shrugged his shoulders in sympathetic agreement.

Looking down at a clipboard in his hand and then to Agent Grant he asked, "What's your blood type?"

"A negative," Phil replied.

"What a coincidence. That's exactly what Officer Monroe is."

Phil was smart enough to know what the medical person was getting to.

"She'll be airlifted to the trauma center at Sandbrook Medical Center. If you like I can call ahead and tell them you'll be coming. It's about a half hour drive from here." The medic waited momentarily for a Phil to respond.

"Yeah, sure, that would be great. I can't promise about the time though, as I'm not sure the police are done with me yet."

The medic turned and started for the ambulance and a look of disgust on his face made Agent Grant feel the need to talk further.

"I'll do the best I can."

Phil walked over to the group of official vehicles now parked in and around the driveway of 39 Gardeners Way. There were two unmarked units and three marked ones, a coroner's van and a crime scene lab truck. He had to step over the yellow crime scene tape, which now encircled the entire property. As he did so, a uniformed officer was about to question him when the sergeant to whom he first spoke intervened.

"He's OK; let him through." Phil continued on his way to where the sergeant and several detectives were standing. A well-dressed short male with thin silver glasses introduced himself.

"Agent Grant, I'm Detective Lance Fresca. I'll be handling this incident. I've already talked to Sgt. Primrose about what you told him. I understand you were in the area on official business."

Agent Grant looked at the sergeant and then back at Detective Fresca.

"Yes, I'm assigned as a protective custody specialist and I was checking on one of our clients in the program. I was leaving the area when Officer Monroe and another officer stopped me as she thought my van was suspicious. By the way, where is the other officer?"

Detective Fresca removed his glasses and rubbed his face as if to clear away any expressions he might be giving. He took a deep breath and said. "He's in the basement. I'm afraid he didn't make it. The shithead that you so effectively dispatched never gave him a chance. It looks like he just emptied his gun into him as he came down the stairs. One of the bullets struck him in the head."

Agent Grant just stood there staring at the detective as if waiting for the information to register. Detective Fresca sensed the effect this had on the agent along with the experience he just went through, but could offer little that would console him. Detective Fresca continued, "Agent Grant, you understand I'll need your service weapon for the forensic team."

"Yes, I figured you would. I just have to notify my superiors of what happened as they will be doing their own investigation in reference to the shooting," Phil said as he retrieved his cell phone out of his pocket and began to dial his office.

Phil got through and relayed the events of the day as he walked away from Detective Fresca. He completed his call and then decided he should call and check on the agents watching Mike Conners.

Chapter 8

Agent Tom Martin sat on the brown chair facing the nurses' station. He enjoyed reading, and this date had two books with him. One was a self-help instruction manual about retirement and the other, a Tom Clancy novel. He was enjoying the Clancy novel and the station nurse, a crusty veteran of twenty-five years, noticed him chuckle.

"What's so funny?" she asked.

The agent didn't look up but continued reading, seemingly oblivious to her question.

"A-hum," the nurse cleared her throat loud enough to get his attention. Glancing up at her and half-smiling he said, "You talking to me?"

"Well, I don't see anyone else here, do you?"

He glanced around and as he did, he noticed the door to Mike Conners' room was open, and standing there peeking out from inside was Mike. As the agent noticed him disappear from view he turned his attention back to the charge nurse.

"How long has Mr. Conners been standing there?" he asked.

The nurse removed her glasses. Peering at the agent she said, "Do you expect me to do your work for you?"

The agent turned slightly red when he realized that she was right. He thought he should be paying more attention to his duties and not indulging himself in other matters. Trying to defend his actions he said, "Never mind, you know it gets kind of boring sitting in one spot with nothing to do but look down a hallway at a closed door."

She managed a slight smile of her own and said, "Tell me about it. I've been at this same station for four years, sometimes with nothing to do for hours at a time." That's about as close as she would come to making the agent feel better about what she said, but then added, "Actually he was watching you for about three minutes."

Agent Martin closed the book and placed it on the table. Shifting his weight as if to get comfortable he said, "Well, I guess reading's out. By the way, when is the next scheduled visit by Dr. Trumbull?"

The nurse glanced at her watch and then at some papers on her desk.

"Well, let's see, it's eleven now, probably sometime between now and four this afternoon."

The agent could sense that she was annoyed by his question but he needed to check on Mr. Conners' condition.

"We couldn't narrow it down a little better, huh?"

"No, we couldn't," she said and went back to her paperwork.

Feeling more uncomfortable than before, Agent Martin stood up and started to walk the edge of the hallway and back again. On his third trip as he turned toward the nurse; he could see her motion for him. He thought, *She's probably going to tell me I'm making her dizzy*. As he got closer, he could see she was holding the phone in her hand.

"Here, it's for you."

"Tom, hi, it's Phil. How's everything going?"

"Slow, very slow," Agent Martin said as he turned his back to the nurse to look down the hall at Mike Conners' room before continuing.

"You were notified that they changed his room, right?"

"No, I wasn't. Why did they do that?"

"The doctor said Mr. Conners' condition had improved to where they didn't want to keep him in that area of the hospital. Actually the room they moved him to is easier to watch him anyway, so it's no big deal."

"Alright then. I was supposed to be there this afternoon, but something came up and I'll be delayed. Probably won't get there until tomorrow."

"Terrific," Tom Martin said, trying not to sound bored. "I don't have anything else to report on as far as Mike Conners condition as the doctor is not scheduled to come in until this afternoon. Also I think he is wondering why I am here, as I caught him looking at me more than once."

"I've given some thought about how to proceed with Mr. Conners. Maybe we should tell him some of the truth as to why we are there. Tell him we are there for his protection until his memory improves. Tell him it's a policy of the hospital, especially under the circumstances of how he was brought in to them. I'd rather have him trust us than be suspicious of why we are there."

"Good," Tom replied. "Do you want me to notify Dr. Trumbull of this?"

"Might as well. I'd contact him myself, but I haven't been able to track him down from here and I'm gonna be real busy for the next several hours."

"Okay, and by the way, what are you tied up on?"

"Oh, just your average everyday burglar gets caught in the act and kills one cop, shoots another and then gets taken out by yours truly."

"Holy shit, you alright?" Tom asked.

"Yeah, just a few scratches and a few hours of initial paperwork and I'll be fine. I'll tell you all about it when I see you."

Tom gave out a low grown and then added, "So, I'll see you when I see you, and don't worry. I'll take care of things on this end."

"Thanks," Phil replied. "I notified Agent Durham also, he'll be there to assist you before I get there."

Agent Martin gave the phone back to the nurse and asked her to contact Dr. Trumbull or Dr. Richards as it was very important that he speak to someone in charge of Mr. Conners.

Three phone calls and some twenty minutes passed before Dr. Richards contacted Tom Martin. The agent discussed his plans with the doctor, who agreed but asked to be present when Mike Conners was informed of the situation.

"That sounds fine with me," Tom said.

It was some time after lunch before Agent Martin found himself standing with Dr. Richards in Mike Conners' room.

As they entered they found Mike sitting on a chair placed in front of the window. He was staring down at the city below and at first, not moving.

"Mr. Conners, are you alright?" asked Dr. Richards.

Mike was startled and jumped up. As he did, the window in front of him vibrated with the intensity of a sonic boom and both men felt a wave of energy which must have felt like a gust of wind push them back slightly.

Agent Martin yelled for Mike to get away from the window, as he ran towards it. When he got there, he realized that it was not open and he looked outside for any sign of an attack. Finding none and turning towards Mike, he became aware that instinctively his service weapon was in his hand. He tried to conceal it in his holster before Mike saw it, but decided it was too late for that and put it away as normal.

"What was that?" Mike said as he looked around the room. Dr. Richards glanced quickly at Agent Martin and then at Mike. Remembering the experience he and Dr. Trumbull had previously with Mike and not wanting anyone else to think that something strange was going on, he said, "That was probably a sonic boom from either the Air Force base or one of those transcontinental jets coming into the airport from overseas. It happens about once a week." He spoke as he walked to the window. The door to Mike's room opened and the charge nurse came in. Dr. Richards noticed that both Mike and Agent Martin looked her way. As they did, he cracked the window open slightly.

"Dr. Trumbull called and said he will be here shortly," she said.

"Thanks, Nurse Belsong," Dr. Richards said and then looked at Agent Martin.

"I've never felt a jet breaking the sound barrier like that before," Tom said.

Dr. Richards looking to add credence to his explanation continued. "The way the airport is situated in the valley it seems to funnel some of the noise in this direction. I have felt similar occurrences before."

"What about the breeze we felt, Doc?" asked Agent Martin.

He turned and pointed towards the window and said, "Well, I guess it's because the window is open slightly."

Agent Martin looked at him suspiciously and walked over to examine it himself. Ted saw him shaking his head and say, "Darndest thing." Before he had a chance to comment further, Dr. Richards started in.

"Mr. Conners, I'd like you to meet Agent Tom Martin from the Federal Bureau of Investigation."

Mike looked at Tom and said, "That explains the gun I saw you put away. I just thought you were some kind of security guard or something."

"Or something," Tom interjected as he shook hands with Mike.

Mike suddenly grew a worried look on his face and sat on his bed. "Why are you here? Did I do something wrong?"

The doctor and agent walked closer to Mike and Tom explained, "You haven't done anything wrong that we know of, Mr. Conners. It's just that we don't know who you are, and it's the policy of the hospital to notify the authorities when such things occur. You of course are aware of the unusual circumstances of how you were located."

"Yes, I see," Mike said.

Agent Martin looked at Mike's hands and continued. "I see that you no longer have the bandages on."

Mike lifted both his hands and looked at them momentarily turning them over several times. "Yeah, I healed pretty fast."

"I'm going to have a technician take your prints to see if you're on file. That might help answer some questions."

Mike felt a pang of uncertainty, which reflected in his face.

"Something wrong, Mr. Conners?" Tom asked.

Mike changed his composure and said, "No, anything that you can do to help me improve my memory is fine with me." As he said this he couldn't help but feel threatened by the agent's remark. He thought about this for a second but couldn't figure out why he felt this way.

Agent Martin also picked up on Mike's change in facial expression and was going to press him further but was interrupted by Dr. Trumbull entering the room.

"Hello, everyone. I got here as fast as I could."

Ted Richards briefed the doctor, leaving out the part about the window.

Dr. Trumbull didn't want Mike to feel that the hospital was hiding something from him and said, "Well, I'm glad the authorities can be of assistance to us and Mr. Conners. If we can find out his identity for certain, with their help, then maybe it would help Mr. Conners with the rest of his memory."

Tom Martin looking at his watch said, "Its two-thirty now. I'll call in and have the technician here within the hour."

Dr. Trumbull looked at his own watch and commented. "That sounds good. What time did you say you had?"

"Two-thirty, Doc."

"My watch must be fast; I have two-thirty-five, actually two-thirty-six."

The agent looked at his watch again and noticed that it still said two-thirty.

Dr. Richards looked at his own watch, which also read two-thirty. He noticed that the second hand was not moving, and an ominous feeling came over him. He suddenly realized that the incident with Mike might have had something to do with it. He did not want the agent to suspect anything unusual and so attempted to hurry along their visit.

"Okay then, Agent Martin, Dr. Trumbull and myself have to discuss another case we are working on, so as soon as the technician arrives, I'll meet you here." He walked toward the door and with his back to Tom, gave Dr. Trumbull a look, the kind of look that says, "Just shut up and play along with me."

Dr. Trumbull didn't say anything and glanced quickly around the room as he walked outside into the hallway with Agent Martin following close behind.

Nurse Belsong looked at Mike who was still sitting on the bed. He let out a small whistle, a small nervous smile on his face.

"Don't let that Mr. Martin worry you none. He seems kind of harmless to me," she said.

"I'm not worried about him. I'm just anxious to see what my prints reveal."

She stared at him, adjusting her glasses as if to get a better look at him.

"You're probably wanted in ten states for various crimes against humanity."

He looked at her, and for a split second thought she was serious. The silence was broken by both of them breaking out in laughter.

"Had you going there for a second, huh," she said.

Talking through a small giggle he replied, "Yeah, that's not really funny though. Could you imagine if it were true?"

The nurse replied, "I consider myself a pretty good judge of character and I don't foresee a problem with you. I've seen a lot of patients faking injuries and illnesses and such. You just don't fit the mold there."

"Thanks for the vote of confidence," Mike said

The nurse replaced the clipboard and said, "Is there anything else I can get for you while I'm free?"

"No, thanks. I'm just going to continue reading the newspapers and maybe watch television for a while. Do you think it would be alright to go for a walk around the hospital?"

"Normally I would say yes, but we have to check with Agent Martin First."

Mike suddenly felt that feeling that he experienced before.

"Well, I'm not a prisoner here, am I?"

Nurse Belsong didn't quite know how to respond to this. She realized that Mike pretty much was a prisoner but didn't want him to feel that way. She attempted to dodge his question by saying, "Now don't start thinking like that. If you were a prisoner, do you think you'd be staying in a room like this?"

Mike mulled this over momentarily before replying, "I see what you're saying, but I still would like to walk around a bit."

Nurse Belsong decided it was time to punt Mike's request to someone other than herself.

"I'll check with the doctors and Agent Martin and let you know." She exited the room before Mike could say anything else.

Mike moved to the small table near the window and pondered what the nurse said. He couldn't help but feel that he was being restrained in some way and a walk would make him feel better. He decided he would wait awhile to see what would be the outcome of his request before taking matters into his own hands. He turned on the television and started to surf the channels for something of interest. He stopped at one channel, which was playing an infomercial.

The friendly bald man was sitting at a comfortable chair, bent over holding a computer disk in his hands. He was pointing to it and explaining how this program would aid a person in learning how to operate a computer. He was giving this program away for free just to get people to try it. As he spoke a list of questions was flashed on the screen with the announcer asking if the viewing audience could correctly answer them. There was a slight pause between question and answer. As each question was asked Mike found himself mouthing the answer just before it was given on the screen. By the fourth question, as he found himself correctly answering each question, it suddenly dawned on him. *I know all of this.* He found himself becoming more excited with each correct answer. The infomercial was over but not Mike's excitement. He walked over and picked up the *Times*. He remembered seeing a section on technology earlier but hadn't read it. One of the articles was titled "Programming Self-Applications for Business." The article had to do with how to use software applications and their source codes for small business applications. Mike began to read and with each paragraph, he realized that he completely understood what was being explained and could have written the article himself. He closed the paper and walked over to the mirror. He stared at his reflection and began to talk to it. "So, Mr.

Conners, you're starting to make yourself known." A small smile crept its way over his face. *I must have worked with computers or programming somewhere in my past. If I could only remember where,* he thought. He sat back down on the chair and grabbed a pencil and paper from the desk drawer. He started to doodle and found himself writing lines of text in numerical sequence, the words were abbreviated and used other symbols between them. After about ten lines he stopped to review his work. A feeling of satisfaction came over him as he realized that he had just written a small computer program to be used for finding an amortization of a mortgage. The excitement of his discovery was too much to keep to himself.

I think I should share this information with Dr. Trumbull, he thought. He was about to reach for the button to summon the nurse, but decided this was the excuse he needed to go for his walk. He glanced out of his room down the hall to where the nurses' station was. He could not see anyone sitting at the desk, but there was Agent Martin sitting on a small sofa, reading a book. Mike stepped into the hall and started for the nurses' desk. The hallway was dimly lit and got brighter as he approached the area where the agent sat. All the way he was looking straight at the area of the desk attempting to see if she was there. From his location he couldn't tell if anyone was at the desk or not as files and paperwork were blocking his view. Agent Martin looked up from the chair where he sat, a puzzled look on his face.

"Is there something I can do for you, Mr. Conners?" he said as he stood up.

"I'm looking for Nurse Belsong; I need to tell her something. Well, actually I need to tell Dr. Trumbull something as soon as she finds him."

"She told me she had to bring some files to the records office and would be right back."

Mike was close enough now to see the nurses' desk and glanced at it and then back to Agent Martin.

"Is there something you want to tell me, and I'll relay it to her?"

"No, I need to speak to the nurse or Dr. Trumbull," Mike said. He couldn't help but feel annoyed at the agent. He didn't really trust him and felt somewhat threatened by his presence.

"Well, then there's nothing much I can do for you, so why don't you go back to your room and I'll relay the message as soon as she gets back."

Mike stood there for a second pondering this. He found himself feeling more like a prisoner than before. He wondered why the nurse would leave without anyone else being there. What if he needed something or suddenly had some kind of seizure or medical emergency? He then remembered his request for a walk.

"Did Nurse Belsong say anything about me wanting to go for a walk?"

Agent Martin's face suddenly changed. He grew a look of annoyance and his voice suddenly became more authoritative.

"Not to me, she didn't. I don't think it's a good idea though, and I really need you to go back to your room," he said.

Mike could feel himself getting more annoyed at the agent's remarks, and a small but growing panic took hold. He shifted his weight several times and turned to look at his room and then back to the nurses' station and then to the agent. Agent Martin sensed this also and his stance changed slightly in response to it.

"Well, can't I just wait here for the nurse?" Mike asked in almost a pleading way as he moved closer to the nurses' desk trying to read the paperwork on it.

Agent Martin moved and positioned himself between Mike and the desk. He was about two inches taller than Mike and about twenty pounds heavier. He raised both hands so as to stop Mike's forward movement.

"Look, I can see you're getting a little upset, and like I said there isn't anything that I can do for you right know, so please go back to your room."

Mike stepped back slightly, looked down at his feet and then back at the agent before replying. "Okay, but I don't understand why you can't let me go for a walk. I mean you can come with me. We'll find the doctor together."

The agent smiled slightly and with a slight grunt answered, "My boss wouldn't like it if I took it upon myself to just go wandering around the hospital with someone I was assigned to keep a watch over, especially if I had no idea where to go to look for the doctor. Anyway you haven't been cleared medically to do that."

"I didn't think I needed clearance. I feel fine, and I really need to speak to the doctor," Mike said. He found himself moving backwards to get the agent out of his personal space.

Tom Martin raised his left hand as if to guide Mike and with his right, he pointed down the hall to Mike's room.

"You're not going anywhere at the moment, and I'm not going to take you on a tour to look for the doctor. So you might as well just go back to your room."

Mike could see he wasn't going to get anywhere with the agent and his frustration level began to rise even further. Ignoring his request, he went instead to the couch where Tom Martin had been sitting. Looking down he saw a book upside down and open so that the front jacket cover and title were visible. He read the words slowly and deliberately in a kind of taunting way just loud enough for the agent to hear.

"*How to Retire Comfortably on One-Thousand Dollars a Month.*" As he read the words he bent down to pick it up but before he could completely grasp control of it, Agent Martin was on him.

"Give me that, and mind your own business," he said as he snatched it from Mike. The force of this caused Mike to lose his balance and fall back on the couch.

"Hey, you don't have to get physical, I was just looking," Mike said. The agent stood over Mike and was clearly upset.

"I don't know what you think you're doing and I asked you nicely to return to your room. I'm not going to ask you again."

A few seconds passed with the agent staring down at Mike and when he didn't move, Agent Martin closed the book and placed it on the table.

Mike wasn't sure what to do next. He couldn't help but feel trapped and as he watched the agent turn slowly towards him, a look of determination and anger on his face, he started to fear for his own safety, a wave of panic took hold. As this happened, Mike began to notice a high-pitched ringing in his ears. He attempted to stop it by shaking his head to no avail. Before he realized it, he was on his feet attempting to get out of the way of the approaching agent. Just before the agent was in reach, Mike raised his hands in self-defense and waited for contact. The sound in his ears was painful, and for the first time he realized that the lighting in the room had suddenly become bluish-green. Not understanding what was happening only heightened his anguish. From Mike's point of view, he could see the agent and the hallway behind him leading to where his room was. This perspective suddenly began to change and it appeared as if the hall was getting longer in size and the agent was moving backwards, slowly at first and then with increasing speed. Mike found himself blinking and squinting his eyes to make sense of what his eyes were telling him and what was really happening. Then suddenly as fast as all this started, it stopped. He stood there facing the hallway, looking around he realized the lighting was as before and the ringing in his ears was gone. The hallway before him appeared empty. The table and chair that were there moments before were gone. Mike tried to analyze what just occurred without immediate success. He raised his hands and called out. "Agent Martin, where are you?" No reply came and Mike's confusion and fear continued. He felt somewhat wobbly and was about to sit down when he noticed the table and chair at the far end of the hall where the door to his room was. Mike started to walk towards them. He was within ten feet of them when a new fear suddenly grabbed him. There on the floor intertwined with them was Agent Martin.

"Oh, shit, what the hell happened?" Mike said to himself. He moved the table away from the agent and attempted to assess his condition. Mike knelt next to him and shook him slightly.

"Agent Martin, are you alright?"

The agent didn't move or respond in any way.

Mike thought, *This can't be happening*. He checked for a pulse on the agent's wrist and thought he felt something but wasn't sure. He stood up and began to pace back and forth in front of his room. Looking again at Agent Martin and the furniture, he found himself panicking with the thought of trying to explain the occurrences of the last few moments and felt for sure that no one would believe his story. He whispered to himself, "I'm totally screwed. I've got to get out of here." Walking over to Nurse Belsong's desk, he found a pen and paper and scratched out a quick note.

> *Dear Dr. Trumbull,*
>
> *Thank you for all your help. I don't know what happened to Agent Martin. I didn't do anything to hurt him. Please don't think badly of me, but I need to find out for myself what happened to me. I will be in touch.*
>
> *Mike Conners*

Walking over to a closet near the elevator, Mike found a blue scrub suit and put it on over his clothes. He then decided to take the stairs down to the basement level. Walking out of the stairwell led him to an area of the boiler room, a rather large room with three huge tanks in front of him and a control room to his left. Mike could see the figure of a man inside. He was bending up and down with pencil in one hand and a clipboard in the other. It appeared that he was inspecting some equipment. The lighting was subdued but Mike could make out a red-lighted sign at the far end which read "Exit." There was a phone on the wall just next to the door. As Mike reached the door, he stopped and discarded the scrubs and picked up the phone. "Yes, may I help you?" came the voice from somewhere within the building.

"There is some kind of emergency on the seventh floor, and a man had an accident and needs a doctor."

"Who is this?" the voice came back. "Hello."

The only response that could be heard by this voice was the sound of the metal door as it shut behind Mike Conners.

Chapter 9

The afternoon heat of the day caught Mike by surprise, and for a split second he had a flashback to his time in the desert. He quickly shrugged it off and climbed the stairs to the street level. He had no idea where he was, but wanted to get as much distance between himself and the hospital as he could. Turning left he saw a street sign that read "S. Maryland Parkway" and started walking towards the corner. He quickly made a right onto Desert Inn Road. He walked at a brisk pace with his head down. He wanted to keep a low profile and found himself looking away from people as they approached. The sun was strong and the air became slightly dusty as he approached an area of construction. The highway department was working on a drainage ditch and the police were assisting with traffic. Mike could feel his pulse quicken as he got closer to them. He wondered how long it would be before there was an all-points-bulletin for his arrest. He passed the intersection at Swenson Street and then the road became a divided highway. He decided to walk on the side facing traffic, so he could better see what was coming. There weren't many cars on his side and he was thankful for that. He could see a red Mustang convertible parked on his side of the road. There was a woman with shoulder-length red hair, wearing a sundress, standing outside of it. Mike thought that she looked a little old to be wearing it. She was talking on a cell phone and waving her right arm in an effort to explain her predicament. Even though he was still about sixty feet from her, he could make out, by the level of her voice, that she was quite upset.

"I don't give a shit that you have a final exam to study for, I need your help," she said.

As Mike got closer, he could see that the car had a flat tire.

"All the times I helped you out and paid for your car insurance and such, you ungrateful bitch, you could at least find your boyfriend and have him come here," she continued. "Sometimes I'm ashamed to call you my daughter."

Mike was just about to the vehicle when the woman's frustrations got the best of her. She began to cry and raised the phone above her head. She looked like a quarterback getting ready to throw the game-winning touchdown in the last-ditch effort with seconds on the clock. Just as she was about to let it fly, she noticed Mike approaching. For a split second the two of them made eye contact. Her arm stopped its forward motion and went limp at her side. A small but noticeable smile formed on her face and she looked slightly embarrassed as she realized she was being watched. The awkwardness of the moment caused Mike to speak.

"Hi, is everything OK?" After he said it, he thought of how stupid it sounded. *Of course not, you jerk. Anyone could see the car had a flat.* He tried to act as though he just noticed the problem and, looking down, said, "Oh, man, a flat."

The woman immediately went into what seemed like a long dissertation of her predicament. About two sentences into her story, Mike raised his hand to stop her.

"Do you want me to change it for you?" he asked.

The woman seemed surprised at his response, but relieved that help was offered.

"Yes, I mean, could you?"

She appeared to be confused that someone, especially a stranger, would be so kind as to stop and offer assistance. Mike sensed her uneasiness and decided it would be a good idea to make her feel better about it.

"I've got some time to kill, and I know how annoying a flat can be. They seem to happen when you least expect them. Where's the jack and spare, in the trunk or underneath?"

"I think they're both in the trunk," she said.

Walking to the rear of the vehicle he waited for her open the trunk. He saw her bend down by the open car door to hit the release and couldn't help but notice her long legs and torso beneath her sundress. He tried to figure her age but couldn't. She had quite a few wrinkles in her face, which made Mike think she was in her late forties, but the rest of her said early thirties. Mike took out the needed items and went to work. The woman moved from the front of her vehicle to the curb adjacent to where Mike was. It was about ninety degrees and the sweat was just started to show up on Mike's forehead when the woman spoke.

"It's so nice of you to help me out, I really appreciate you doing this for me."

She said this in a way that made Mike feel she was not used to asking for help or was wealthy enough to not have had many of this type of problem. He stopped momentarily and looked up at her.

"Not a problem, Miss…" He hesitated long enough to make her realize that a formal introduction might be called for.

"Oh, I'm sorry. My name is Melissa Borjon. It's French, not that it matters, but people after hearing me say it usually ask." Mike was amused by her sudden candor.

"The thought never occurred to me."

"This is not my car. My daughter and I switched this morning. I think she wanted to impress some boy and get her boyfriend jealous. I never expected to break down."

Mike stopped to look at her before replying.

"It's not that big a deal. Just think, you saved your daughter from going through the aggravation. The way this tire looks, no matter who drove the car, it probably would have happened."

Mike was just tightening the lugs when he heard a male voice ask, "Is everything alright?"

"Yes, Officer," Melissa replied.

Mike felt a twinge of uneasiness roll through his body as he heard a car door slam and the footsteps of the officer approaching. He didn't look up but slowed to complete the tightening of the lugs.

The officer walked to where she was standing and took a look at Mike's progress.

"Are you going to be much longer?" he asked. Mike didn't look up and replied, "Be about three more minutes."

"Your vehicle is kind of parked a little too far from the side of the road. The next time you get a flat, try to pull off the road more."

Mike glanced quickly at the officer and couldn't help but notice he was more interested in Melissa's legs than in him or the Melissa's vehicle.

"That's my fault, Officer. I was driving, and you're right, next time, if there ever is one, I'll be more careful," Melissa said.

The officer gestured with his hand to his hat briefly and said, "Have a nice day."

Mike felt relieved he left and hurried to finish his task. He placed the flat tire in the trunk and was about to close it when Melissa said, "Here is a rag to wipe your hands." She stood as he cleaned them and continued. "I don't know how to thank you. Can I take you somewhere? I mean do you live locally?"

Mike was caught off-guard by her question and didn't want to sound suspicious. He looked down the road at a billboard and said, "Oh, wow, thanks. Yeah I'm staying at the Excalibur on the Strip. I had taken a cab to the Convention Center and was walking back when I saw you." Mike didn't know if she bought his story or not but it was the only one he could come up with at the moment.

"Great!" she said. "Get in."

Mike opened the passenger door and got in. As the car moved down the road and passed the billboard, Mike looked up at it. He saw the picture of a castle with flags unfurling in the wind and words beckoning the public to have an adventure while at Vegas in a castle made for the whole family. The Excalibur truly looked like a fun place to stay. Mike managed a small smile as he turned to look at his new friend.

The car radio was tuned to a country and western station and Mike could hear Melissa humming to it. Sitting there driving with the sun in her hair and the wind tugging at her sundress, lifting it ever so slightly to reveal her smooth thighs aroused Mike's feelings a little.

"Do you like country and western music?" he asked.

"It depends. My tastes vary from day to day. Today, with the weather warm and sunny, driving with the top down, I just feel country," she said as she threw him a smile with her glance.

Mike looked away at the barren mountains way in the distance and said, "Sure is beautiful."

"Excuse me?"

"The mountains. The mountains are beautiful," Mike said, trying to accentuate the word "mountain."

Melissa giggled slightly and said, "Oh, yeah, the mountains."

Her voice trailed off as she spoke, and Mike wondered what she was thinking.

"So, where are you from, Mr. Conners?"

Mike found himself feeling uneasy again and blurted out, "Chicago, I'm here on a mini vacation."

"Married, children?" she asked.

Mike was taken by surprise by her sudden questions. He didn't want to sound rude but found himself suddenly getting annoyed at the idea of making stuff up.

"I'm a widower." The words came out and Mike couldn't figure out why he said it. He didn't even know who he was. He realized that the more he lied the easier it was to make a mistake and be caught in it. He decided to go on the offensive.

"What about you? I know you have a daughter. Is there a husband?"

"Yeah, there's a husband, if you want to call him that. He is so busy half the time with his business—" She stopped momentarily to shrug he shoulders and cock her head. "I hardly see him."

Mike thought about not only what she said, but also how she said it.

Judging by how she acted to this point, he felt that if she weren't ripe for an affair, she soon would be.

"What kind of business is he in?" Mike asked.

"He has a private plane and courier service out at McCarran Airport. If he is not flying some celebrity around, he's transporting diamonds and such to various places."

"That sounds like an exciting and lucrative job."

"It might be for him, but not for me. The money is good and all, but hugging a bag of money is not the same as having companionship."

Mike felt that the conversation was getting too personal and he couldn't afford that now. She continued talking about her relationship and as Mike listened, he suddenly felt a strange but familiar feeling of having a similar conversation in the past. He didn't know with whom, but a lot of the words sounded the same. He looked at her, with the glare of the sun and the wind in her hair and as she spoke, her appearance seemed to change. The red became blond and her wrinkles faded. Her voice seemed to get smoother. He found himself mouthing and thinking her name. "*Melissa.*"

Mike blinked several times and shook his head for the scene to change. When all was normal, Mike suddenly realized she was looking at him.

"Mr. Conners, are you alright?"

"Ah, yeah," he replied.

"I was talking to you when suddenly you got this blank look on your face. You look like you saw a ghost or something. I apologize. I'm sure you don't need to hear my problems."

Mike didn't know what to say. He was visibly shaken and couldn't understand what he just experienced.

"No, it's quite alright, I guess the sun got to me for a second or something."

"Well, that's a relief. You got all pale looking," Melissa said.

Mike looked away out his window and continued to think about this. The vision he saw seemed very familiar but he couldn't figure out who she was but knew it must be someone from his past, someone probably important to him. He tried to focus his memory to picture this person again in his mind, without success.

Melissa made a left onto Las Vegas Boulevard. They traveled on in silence for about a minute before she started with her questions once again.

"So, how long will you be staying in Vegas?"

This time Mike didn't think she was being nosy but was just asking to ease the awkwardness of the moment.

"Probably a week. It depends if I get bored."

"Bored! I don't see how anyone could stay in Vegas and be bored. There are enough things to do here to fill ten vacations." The sound of her voice almost made Mike feel she was defending the city.

"I don't mean bored in the traditional sense. I know there's plenty to do. It's just that how many times can you play the slots or craps or whatever. After all, isn't that why most people come here?"

"Yeah, I guess, but there is a lot more to do than that. You should try going to the desert. There are some really pretty sights out there."

Mike didn't know how to respond to this. If she only knew he already had his fill of the desert. In fact when he looked out into it from where he sat the thought of it made him shudder.

The traffic began to get heavier as they made their way toward the heart of the strip. Along the way they passed the New Frontier, Treasure Island and the Mirage Casinos. Mike had never been to Vegas. At least he had no recollection of having gone there. He noticed that even in the heart of the day, with the bright sun shining down, the place seemed like one big party. He could see people walking along and staring at the structures with a childlike look of anticipation. He had to admit with each casino that they passed, he too became excited about what might be inside.

They continued south along Las Vegas Boulevard passing Flamingo Road. As they passed the Bellagio, Melissa couldn't help but comment on it.

"That's probably the nicest casino in Vegas. A little on the expensive side to stay there, but very exquisite." Mike thought about this for a second before responding.

"I guess you've been to every casino in town, huh?"

"Not every one. There are about twenty-four of them on the Strip alone. I probably have been in at least fifteen of them." As she said this, Mike noticed a small smile break her concentration of driving. "I have some nice memories of some and some bad ones of others," she said. Mike didn't want to appear nosy, but this statement made him more curious about her. He decided a little more information might be in order.

"Oh, so I guess the bad ones come from not winning that day," Mike said as he shifted in his seat to face her more.

Melissa stopped at a traffic light and as she did, she turned to look at him. Her eyes met his and by the look on her face Mike could sense that she wanted to say something, but was searching for the right words. When she finally did speak it was slow and deliberate.

"No, at least not losing in the traditional sense. I used to work the casinos." She waited for a reaction.

At first Mike thought he didn't hear her completely. Then he realized that she left out the word "in" before the word casinos. That's when it hit him.

"Ooh!" he said at the very same time as she said, "Yeah," in a drawn-out phrase that told her he understood what she meant.

"It was a time in my life that I'm not proud of. I was new to the area, had no money or place to stay. I became involved with the wrong people. It was only after I met my husband, Richard, that things changed. He was different from other people. He treated me like a real person and not just a quick lay." After she said this she stopped herself. Mike could see a far-off, hurt look in her eyes.

"Hey, everyone gets down on their luck from time to time. I can remember when I did things that I regretted later on." This of course was a lie. Mike couldn't recall much of anything about his past, but felt a need to console her. The light changed and they proceeded. Another minute went by in silence, and Mike was about to ask about her daughter just to change the subject when they arrived in front of the Excalibur.

"Well, here we are," Melissa said. She pulled up past the valet parking area, and out of the way of other vehicles so they could get by. An energetic attendant ran up to the vehicle and was waved off by Melissa.

She put the car in park and turned to Mike.

"I don't know how to thank you," she said as she fumbled through her pocketbook.

"Don't worry about it," he replied and as he reached for the door, she pulled on his arm.

"Wait, please take this. It's the least I can do." Her other hand extended out holding a folded bill.

"No, I couldn't. It was only a flat tire. Anyone could have changed it. No big deal," he said as he squeezed her hand shut and started to exit his side the car.

She got this cutesy look about her, and retreated out her side of the car. She met him as he turned from closing his door and pulled him into an embrace of thanks. Kissing him softly on the cheek and said, "Thanks again. If you're ever in need of an escort, here is my husband's card."

Mike looked at it briefly before putting it in his pocket.

"Take care and thanks for the ride," he said as he moved to the walkway for the entrance to the casino. He paused and turned around to watch her as she drove off. His chance meeting with Melissa was a nice reprieve from his other troubles, but as soon as she was out of view, he knew he must turn his attention once again to his biggest problem. As he stood there contemplating his next course of action, the valet once again attempted to offer some assistance.

"Sir, you look lost. Can I help you?"

"Ahhh, no thank you, I'm just trying to decide what I want to do. Which way to the main lobby?"

"Through those doors to your left and then straight down the hall, you'll come to a big casino area. It should be to your right from there."

Mike thanked him and proceeded through the doors and on to the main lobby. He didn't know why he was headed there, but for the lack of something better to do. Anyway he decided he was here so he might as well check it out. As he walked along the hall, the atmosphere of the place amused him. The walls and floor were decorated and made one feel as though you were in a real castle. The employees of course were wearing the garb of that era, and two larger-than-life knights in full battle dress guarded the entrance to the casino hall. As he entered the casino area he could see off to his right the long counter that had hotel personnel stationed behind it to assist the customers. Mike thought it odd that they did not wear medieval garb but instead were dressed in red sports jackets and white shirts. The atmosphere of the casino itself was more like an amusement park than a place to gamble, especially with all the children running around. As he approached the line of people waiting to be served, he again began to think about the day's events. He found himself especially worried about the events that occurred at the hospital. He decided to make an attempt to call Dr. Trumbull and check on the condition of Agent Martin. He didn't have any change, but maybe the front desk would let him use the house phone. His only concern about this was if the call was somehow traced to his location. He thought about this for a second and decided it would be all right as long as the conversation didn't linger.

Mike waited in line behind a well-dressed man wearing a double-breasted dark suit and the shiniest shoes he ever saw. The man carried a black attaché case in one hand and a cell phone in the other. Mike took him to be an accountant or lawyer. As Mike stood there listening to the rhythmic sounds of the slots from the casino floor, he heard what he thought was a song playing. Looking down at the man's hand he thought it was his cell phone. He wasn't quite sure but after about the third chorus, Mike tapped him on the shoulder and said, "I think your phone is ringing." The man raised the phone to eye level, looked at the screen and then at Mike.

"No, I think you're mistaken. See it's not even on, but I guess it should be. I'm playing hooky from work today, and I didn't want anyone to bother me." With that he pressed the "on" button and placed the phone in his front top pocket of his suit jacket. Mike found himself looking around and trying to figure out where the song had come from. There was no one on line behind him. There wasn't even anyone within ten feet of him. He began to get annoyed at himself and thought of how stupid he must have sounded to the man on line with him. Mike was about to apologize when he heard the song once again. This time though, Mike saw the man jump slightly in response to it.

"Oh, man, I think you jinxed me."

Mike heard the ring and realized it was the same tune again. The man looked at the screen for a second before commenting.

"Just what I thought." He smiled, looked at Mike and said, "I'm not going to answer it." Once again he placed it in his pocket.

Mike thought, *Well, I hope it's not important.*

A few seconds went by and the phone rang again with the same tune as before. Mike knew the man heard it as he flinched with each successive bar of music that was played. This was a little curious to Mike, but the thing that was most curious was the song itself. It seemed oddly familiar to him, but he didn't know why.

This song and the reaction went on a third time before Mike could no longer contain his curiosity.

"Excuse me," he said. "I hope you don't think I'm nosy, but what is the name of that song your phone keeps playing?"

The man gave Mike a look of disgust. And as he finally reached to answer it he said, "Unchained Melody."

The sound of the answer caught Mike like a cold wind, and he gasped slightly. *I knew it sounded familiar,* he thought. In fact it was more than just familiar. Mike knew this song had a special meaning. He began to replay the song in his mind trying to attach it to some other part or time in his life. There was something there, but it was just out of his reach. This memory crap was really starting to frustrate him. He could feel his anger growing and didn't know what to do about it. He wanted to understand what had happened to him in the past and what was happening now. There were too many weird and unexplainable things going on and he knew eventually he would need help to figure them out. He found himself going over in his mind the little things that happened till now and questioned them. How can someone hear what a person is thinking if they're not actually saying it, as with Nurse Farley. How can someone hear a phone ring when it's not even on? The biggest and scariest event was how does one move people and furniture down a hall without touching them? Mike knew that the only people capable of understanding all of this were at the hospital from which he so wanted to distance himself; the same people who by now probably wanted to prosecute him.

Mike could hear the conversation between the man and his office. Judging by the tone in his voice, Mike figured someone was getting into trouble, but it didn't appear it was going to be the man. Mike figured he was the boss or at least in charge, as the man began barking orders to not be disturbed and such.

"I don't care what the district manager said. I'm not ready to make that decision yet. I'll let you know when I return," the man said.

After a slight pause, he continued. "Fine then, wait, let me write down the number." The man fumbled, retrieved a pen from his pocket and then continued looking through his other pockets. When he didn't find what he needed, he turned to Mike and asked, "Do you have a piece of paper on you?"

Mike knew he didn't, but to be courteous, he started searching his pockets.

"No, I don't believe I do," he said.

"Wait, what's this?" Mike said as he felt something in his right pocket that felt like paper. His hand came out holding a fifty-dollar bill.

"Thanks anyway," the man replied, "but I don't think it's that important." He laughed slightly and left the line to retrieve a piece of paper from the front desk.

Mike stood there momentarily trying to figure out how he came in possession of the bill. A small smile emerged from his lips as he remembered the hug he received from Melissa just before she left him. *That little son of a gun, she must have slipped it in my pocket as she hugged me.* Mike was not expecting anything for his services when he changed her tire. Melissa had other ideas though. He stuck the money back in his pocket and decided to get off the line for the front desk and go to the change window in the casino. On the way there he had to walk right through the middle of the casino. The sights and sounds of the people playing the various games, some yelling and cheering and the sound of the slots with their bells keeping a constant beat, were somewhat hypnotic. Mike could see how easily a person could get hooked on the atmosphere alone. Everything was designed to make you feel good about being there and good about spending money with the possibility of getting rich.

Mike got change for his fifty and proceeded to a bank of pay phones near by. He was surprised to see that there were only three phones there. The casino owners probably felt that in this day and age most people had their own cell phones with them, so why waste floor space on phones when you could use it for slot machines?

He called information and got the number for the hospital. He dialed and was confronted with a long list of menu options. None of them really listed doctors, just departments with other sub-menus to try. He decided to just try pressing zero and when he did a live voice finally picked up.

"Hello, Reception. May I help you?"

"Yes, I'm trying to reach Dr. Trumbull. I don't know what his extension is."

"One moment, please. I'll connect you to his secretary."

Mike waited patiently for the operator to connect him. After about two minutes a woman answered. "Dr. Trumbull's office."

"Yes, my name is—" Mike stopped in midstream when he realized that he couldn't give his true name. Thinking as quickly as he could he blurted out, "Mike Jeffries. It's very important that I speak with Dr. Trumbull as soon as possible."

"Dr. Trumbull is a way from his desk at the moment. May I take a message?"

Mike didn't know how to respond to this. He wanted to speak to the doctor and find out how Agent Martin was and in the process assure the doctor that what happened wasn't his fault. He couldn't really leave a message or anything traceable, so he decided to try back later.

"No, but when do you think would be a good time to catch the doctor in?" he asked.

"Usually between nine and eleven in the morning. After

that…" She paused and Mike could hear her muffled voice talking as her hand covered the phone.

"Hello," Mike said.

"Mr. Jeffries, one moment please, I see the doctor coming in now."

Mike waited again. He could feel his pulse quicken as an uneasy feeling rose up from within. He felt it was taking to long, but stopped the urge to hang up. He was just about to lose the battle when he heard a familiar voice.

"Hello, this is Dr. Trumbull. May I help you?"

The sound of his voice startled Mike and he didn't answer.

"Hello!" came the voice again.

"Dr. Trumbull, this is Mike."

At first the doctor didn't recognize the voice and said, "Yes. My receptionist told me there was a Mike Jeffries on the phone. What can I do for you."

"No, Doc, it's Mike Conners. I didn't want to give my real name before I had a chance to speak to you."

"Mr. Conners, where the heck are you? You had me and Dr. Richards worried."

"I don't think it's a good idea for me to say at the moment. How is Agent Martin?"

"He has a slight concussion, but he'll be alright. And I think you have a little explaining to do about what happened."

"That's a little hard to say, as I'm not sure myself," Mike said.

"You created quite a mess in the hallway on the ward, and the FBI has been a pain in the ass since. They've been questioning everyone they see to figure out what happened and where you are."

"What did Agent Martin tell them?" Mike asked.

"I don't know what he told them, but when I asked, he said one minute he was trying to get you to go back to your room, and the next thing he knew, he was flying through the air."

Mike told Dr. Trumbull about the events just prior to his leaving. He also told him about his memory of working with computers.

There was a slight pause between the two and then the doctor continued.

"Mike, I don't know if you realize it or not, but there are things that are happening to you that are not exactly normal. Things aside from your loss of memory that we should look into in a controlled environment. We need to find out more about these things before someone really gets hurt."

"I know," Mike said. "I just don't like the controlled environment part. I think if I can just get more of my memory back, then it would help a great deal."

"I agree, but I also feel you have a better chance here at the hospital than wandering around Las Vegas."

Mike thought about this for a moment before replying. "Even if I came back to the hospital, I don't think the FBI would allow me to stay there."

"I think I can straighten things out with them to allow you to stay in the hospital's custody."

Mike started to say something, as he heard the doctor mumbling something in the background. He realized that he was on the phone way too long for comfort.

"Listen, I know your intentions are good, but I'm not ready to do that just yet. I'll keep in touch. Good-bye."

"Wait!" the doctor said, but it was too late. Mike was already walking through the casino towards the exit.

Chapter 10

Dr. Trumbull sat with the phone still in his hand for a good minute before hanging it up. He didn't know if he should inform the FBI about speaking to Mike. He was torn between helping his patient and performing his civic duty. His Hippocratic belief won out and he would keep silent. He picked up the phone again and told his secretary to page Dr. Richards. A few minutes later, his door opened and Ted Richards said, "What's up?"

"Come in and close the door." By the sound of his voice Ted knew this would not be your typical meeting. Ted moved to the red leather chair stationed in front of the doctor's desk, sat down and crossed his legs. "Okay?"

"I just received a phone call from Mike Conners."

"What!"

Without commenting on Ted's surprise, Alex continued. "He's alright. He called out of concern for Agent Martin."

Ted had a look on his face. A look that said he had many questions. Alex told him what was said and about the suggestion of coming back.

"He's not ready to come back, but the longer he stays away, the more trouble he's apt to get into," Alex said.

"Well, did he give you any indication as to where he was calling from? I mean he hasn't been gone that long and couldn't have gotten too far."

"He wouldn't say, but there was a lot of background noise. It sounded like he was in a casino."

"Terrific, well that narrows it down to thirty or so places," Ted said. "What do you want to tell the FBI?"

Dr. Trumbull looked up quickly from his desk at Ted with a look of surprise. Ted knew this look, knew what it meant, and also knew it could get them into serious trouble with the authorities.

"I agree," were the only words that came out of Ted's mouth.

The two of them knew they were Mike's best chance at finding out about his past and maybe getting his life back.

"Do you want to drive around and look for him?" Ted asked.

"You can if you like. I think I should stay here in case he calls back."

"I know it would be like looking for a needle in a haystack, but maybe I can try the bigger casinos," Ted added. "I don't really have anything pressing today anyway."

Ted stood up and was about to leave, when Dr. Trumbull's secretary opened the door.

"Excuse me, Doctors. There's an Agent Grant from the FBI in the lobby who insists on speaking with you."

"Thank you; tell him I'll be right with him."

She closed the door, and Ted said, "I'll keep in touch."

He walked to the door and was about to open it when it opened for him.

Phillip Grant stood there with a serious look of distrust on his face. Before Ted could say "Excuse me," Agent Grant said, "Ah, just the two men I've been looking for. Stay awhile, won't you!" As he said this, he raised his hands to guide Ted back into the room.

Dr. Trumbull stood up and moved from behind his desk. "What's going on, Agent Grant?"

"It's so hard to track you guys down. It seems you're never in the same place at the same time."

"We're very busy men. Agent Grant. What is it you need?"

Agent Grant walked over to the same chair Ted just left. From this vantage point he could see and read the papers on Dr. Trumbull's desk. As he looked down his voice slowed as he continued. "I just wanted to ask the two of you if anyone has any idea where Mr. Conners might be."

Dr. Trumbull resented the intrusion and with a raised voice said, "Agent Grant, I've already told you I don't have any idea as to where he might be. And I can honestly say that if any of my staff knew something, they would surely come forward to help."

As he said this he knew it was a lie, at least a partial lie, but a lie nevertheless. He only hoped it sounded believable enough. Agent Grant looked at both doctors like a person at an art gallery staring at a painting trying to analyze it. The uncomfortable moment caused Dr. Trumbull to shudder inside. He hated lying and turned to Dr. Richards for relief.

"Dr. Richards, do you have anything to tell Mr. Grant?"

Ted Richards looked at his partner with a look of disdain. *Oh, sure, throw me to the wolf,* he thought. "No, I don't. We've searched the whole hospital without success, so he must have left."

Dr. Trumbull could see the look on the agent's face, which clearly said he didn't completely believe them. He also knew that no matter what was said, the agent would be skeptical.

"I'm still not sure if this Mr. Conners is the man I'm hoping him to be, as I wasn't able to get his prints before this happened. I just hope the two of you realize how important it is that we find him. I'll be in touch," he said as he moved towards the door.

Agent Grant walked out of the office leaving the door open

and proceeded down the hall to the elevator. He glanced back once to see Dr. Richards close the door and stay inside. He wondered what they were saying and thought about bugging the office but decided against it for now. As he waited for the elevator, he called Bob Durham to figure out their next move. The elevator opened and Phil moved inside the empty chamber for the ride to the main lobby.

"Bob, it's Phil."

"What's up?"

"Not much. Were you able to get any fingerprints off of anything in the hallway of the hospital?"

"We got a partial off of the desk by the nurses' station and another from the room Mr. Conners was in. as soon as I hear from the lab, I'll let you know."

"Good. Also I want to put a tail on both Dr. Richards and Dr. Trumbull."

"Why? Do you think they're hiding this guy somewhere?"

"No, but I think they know something or have information that they don't want me to know about."

"Do you want a wire also?" Bob asked.

"I wasn't gonna, but yeah, maybe we will. Also I want the phone log of all calls coming and going for Dr. Trumbull starting with yesterday."

"Okay! I'll get right on it. Where are you going now?"

"I thought I'd take a ride around a bit, maybe get something to eat before I go back to see Tom Martin again."

"Yeah, I spoke with him earlier. He's got quite a headache."

The two agents disconnected just as the elevator door opened to the lobby. Agent Grant walked out the doors through the lobby and the front entrance. The heat of the day was oppressive and on his way to his car, he decided to get rid of his jacket and tie.

Chapter 11

Mike Conners looked back once at the phone he just left and thought about his conversation with Dr. Trumbull. He was relieved to hear that Agent Martin's injury was not life-threatening. He had a strong urge to keep moving but wasn't sure just why. He knew that the FBI was now looking for him and thought that was a good reason to feel this way, but there was something else, something that he couldn't put his finger on. The harder he tried the more frustrated it became for him.

As he walked on, the sights and sounds of the casino began eroding his frustrations. He stopped at a roulette table to watch as the people placed their bets on the numbers. He stood next to an Oriental man in his thirties who was placing five-dollar chips haphazardly all over the table. He was practically knocking other people out of the way in the process. Mike counted ten spots that were occupied by his money. The wheel was spun and the ball stopped on number thirty-one black. No one won and Mike could hear the man say something in his own tongue. As soon as he was allowed, the man again placed ten five-dollar bets throughout the table in no certain order. Again the ball came to rest. This time on sixteen red.

"Yes!" the man exclaimed as he pumped his fist in the air.

"How much did you win?" Mike asked. The man didn't look at Mike but said in broken English, "One hundred seventy-five dollar."

"Good for you," Mike added.

Still not looking at Mike, he said, "I up now seventy-five dollar."

After watching the man win and lose a few times, Mike found himself silently betting on numbers to himself as the real action continued before him. Seven red, then twenty-eight black, then twenty-two black. Mike began to hear a slight humming in his head. He didn't notice at first as he was getting caught up in the betting. He wasn't actually betting, but the numbers he was picking began to come in more frequently. When he could no longer ignore the humming, he stepped away from the table and shook his head slightly and looked around for the source of this sound. The humming stopped and Mike was left to wonder if he wasn't having some sort of physical relapse. It wasn't painful when it occurred, just annoying. He moved back to the table and started his silent betting once again. The longer he stayed, the more consistently right his number picking became. The humming returned, but not as loud as the first time.

A deep excitement began to take hold of Mike as he realized what was happening was not mere chance or good luck, but some new ability that he had. He wanted to try it out for real. He purchased forty dollars' worth of chips and decided to use it to make eight separate five-dollar bets. If he couldn't come out ahead by then, he would just chalk it up to bad luck and move on.

Mike's first bet was on twenty-three red. He waited as the wheel spun and the silver ball was propelled by the dealer in the opposite direction. It made its way around several times before succumbing to the force of gravity and bouncing to rest on Eight

Black. Mike looked at it sitting there. The number eight was right next to his selection. He grunted slightly and waited, scanning the wheel, looking for his next bet. His eyes settled on number fourteen red. He would look away but found himself going back to it. He placed his chip on it and waited once again for the results. This time the ball bounced several times before coming to a stop on his number. He heard the Dealer say, "Fourteen red." At first it didn't register. The sight of his ball sitting in the slot was exciting and a little unnerving to Mike. He watched as the dealer moved one hundred and seventy dollars' worth of chips in front of him. He scanned the wheel for his next bet and tried again with the same results. Mike figured it was time to up the ante a little; this time he moved a ten dollar chip to the slot for two black. He waited and almost fell off his chair when the ball settled onto his number. The dealer once again moved chips, this time totaling three hundred and fifty dollars in front of Mike.

The dealer said, "Place your bets." But Mike didn't move. The Oriental man next to him waited momentarily and turned to Mike and said, "What you waiting for, you be hot, keep going." Mike was stunned and still didn't move. He slowly looked at the man and finally spoke.

"I'm sorry, are you talking to me?"

"Yes, you be very lucky now. I wait for you to bet and play what you play."

Mike suddenly noticed other people at the table were also looking at him. A slight feeling of paranoia began to take hold and Mike knew it was time to leave.

"I'm sorry, I don't want to press my luck." He got up, collected his winnings and left the table. As he walked away, he could hear the groans from the other players. Mike went to the first men's room he could find and proceeded to splash cold water on his face. Taking a deep breath he stood and stared at his reflection in the mirror. *Shit, this is incredible,* he thought. He had won over five hundred dollars. He kept thinking that this must be some sort of rare good luck. How else could he have known what numbers were going to come up? *Unless I somehow made the ball land in those positions,* he thought. He thought about what he did and started thinking about the other strange events that he was involved with since his rescue in the desert. He had no explanation for them, yet they did occur. He remembered Dr. Trumbull's suggestion for returning to the hospital and again dismissed it from his mind. He decided to try something else to see if his theory held water.

Mike left the men's room and headed straight for the crap tables. There were two rows of tables with six tables in each row. There was plenty of space between tables and Mike figured that was to accommodate as many players as possible. He decided on the last table, as there were the fewest people there. There were five people around the table but only two of them were actually playing. He stood next to a tall lean man, dressed in jeans and sneakers. The man had a rough voice with a Southern drawl. There was a beautiful blonde to his right egging him on. She looked too young for him, but what the heck, this was Vegas. She could have been just an escort. Mike started by just observing the action and watching the rolls of the dice. He tried telling himself what numbers would come up. He discovered that out of ten tries, he only got three right. Hardly a success. He decided to try to concentrate on a particular number rather then just guessing. He started with the number six. On the third roll of the dice, it came up. Mike decided to stick with this number, which hit again on the very next roll. *Okay,* he thought, *one more time.* A third time, the number six came out. A feeling of success swept over him. It was then that he realized that he had some sort of telekinetic ability. He tried different numbers and was successful nine out of ten tries. He also noticed that the hum in his head returned the more he concentrated. Mike moved to a position that would assure him a turn at the dice. Purchasing some chips, he placed them on several numbers and the pass line. He did this mainly to cover up his real bet, which this time was the number four. The shooter to his right shook the dice several times and said, "Come on, baby, do it for me." He let them fly out across the table to the far end where they came to rest.

"Four!" the stickman yelled, and Mike couldn't help but smile.

The dealer quickly cleared the table of the losers and paid out to the winners. The next number Mike decided on was nine, which made him a winner again. The excitement of the moment was incredible. The more Mike played, the more he won. Finally after several rolls of the dice, it was Mike's turn. He noticed his hands became moist with anticipation. He rubbed them on his pant legs and thought of a number. He was trying not to appear too obvious, betting small amounts and including losing numbers on purpose. He wanted to maintain control of the dice long enough to prove this wasn't just some strange fluke. As long as he didn't crap out by rolling a two, three, or twelve, he'd be good.

He placed a bet for the number two as snake eyes. He rolled the dice and the first die came to a rest showing one spot. The second die stopped on a two, for a split second, but then the strangest thing happened. All of a sudden it rolled over one final time with the number one clearly showing. The stickman caught himself just in time, and with a look of astonishment said, "Snake eyes!" Yells of excitement from the other players along with the realization of his success were somewhat intoxicating to Mike. The more he played the more he won and he was clearly getting caught up in the moment.

On the casino floor at any one time there are several employees who do nothing but watch the action. The main person in charge is called the pit boss. John Sensor was one of these people. Mr. Sensor and his assistant stood for a while observing Mike. Finally Mr. Sensor who spoke without taking his eyes off of Mike said, "What do you think?"

The assistant, a short, pudgy man in his late forties, didn't answer at first. When he finally spoke, it was in small choppy phrases. "Ah, I don't know. I've never seen a run of luck. I mean if it is luck. I don't know, what do you think?"

"Well, what's he up by?"

"My guess is ten thousand."

The boxman is an employee of the casino who sits at the table next to the dealer or stickman. Mr. Sensor moved to a position in front of the boxman to get his attention. When he looked up at Mr. Sensor, he was given the signal to change the dice. Before the very next roll the dice were changed and the pit boss moved back to his original position to continue watching. Even before the outcome of the next roll of the dice were known, the dice were being taken to an area of the casino to be tested to make sure that they weren't modified in any way. Casinos pride themselves in keeping the games honest and when the laws of probability seem to be challenged, they move to examine why as soon as they can.

People who frequent casinos are a funny bunch. A lot of them are drawn to the play by the excitement of the win. Yelling and cheering in the excitement of the moment causes others to be attracted to it like some weird feeding frenzy. As Mike continued to play, winning more than losing, the small group of players originally there started to grow. It wasn't long before the size of the crowd and their enthusiastic behavior snapped Mike out of his trance-like state.

He looked around and realized he had become the center of attention. This was not good and a small fear of discovery crept up on him. He had a great urge to get up and leave but thought better of it. That in itself would bring more attention to him. He looked down at his chips and for the first time became aware of the large sum he had won. The crowd around him started to get impatient, as Mike was not rolling the dice. He looked at the dice in his hand and then up at the stickman.

"I think I've had enough for one day," he said and placed the dice on the table in front of him. Some boos and sighs could be heard coming from the others who were betting and winning along with him. As Mike looked around he felt as if some of the people were staring right through him. Some of them actually appeared to have a look of anger or contempt. One of the spectators, a short, stocky man in his late forties, was eyeing him in a particularly strange way that gave Mike a feeling of impending doom. The man had a cell phone in one hand and raised it to make a call. Before he could connect, an employee tapped him on the shoulder.

"Excuse me, sir, but cell phone calls are not allowed in the gaming area." The stocky man gave the employee a look of disgust, glanced Mike's way and then walked off. Mike was somewhat relieved to see him leave, as he appeared to be studying him more than the others. Mike didn't look at him directly, as he didn't want to appear challenging.

The stickman maneuvered the dice away from Mike with his stick and onto the next player. Mike started to count and collect his chips when Mr. Sensor touched him on the shoulder.

"Excuse me, sir, my name is John Sensor, I'm an employee of the casino."

Mike stopped and looked at him. Mr. Sensor smiled and continued. "That's quite a pile of money you've collected."

Mike looked down at his winnings and then back to Mr. Sensor. "Yes, I guess it is."

"May I make a suggestion Mr.—" He hesitated to wait for a reply.

"It's Mike, Mike Conners," Mike said as he extended his hand to introduce himself.

"Well, Mr. Conners. First the management of the casino would like to congratulate you on your fortunate play," John Sensor said as he adjusted a small earpiece. "Excuse me a second." He took a step back and Mike could clearly see he was listening to someone. The hotel security office was on the other end.

"Mr. Sensor, the dice check out. There is nothing unusual about them."

"Thank you."

Mr. Sensor turned his attention back to Mike and with somewhat of a friendlier smile said, "I was about to suggest that you allow us to change your winnings into a check for any amount up to your winnings that you like."

He paused momentarily. "For security reasons."

Mike looked around and noticed some of the other players still had their eyes on him. A small feeling of paranoia began to take hold. He looked back at Mr. Sensor with a look that telegraphed his feelings.

Mr. Sensor said, "I don't mean to worry you, but it's just a service we like to provide. Are you staying here at the hotel?"

"Ah, no, no, I'm not. Does it matter?" Mike asked.

"No, not at all; in fact, I'd like to offer you a free room from the casino for up to three days, if you'd like."

Mike was startled by the offer and was about to ask why when John Sensor continued.

"You see, the management likes to keep their customers happy. And we like to reward good luck. If it's not a room you need then I can offer you tickets to a show or free meals or whatever."

Mike thought about this for a moment and a big smile suddenly crossed his face.

"Oh, I get it now, you want me to stick around and maybe I'll give back some by playing some more," he said with a chuckle.

"That is entirely possible, but up to you," John said, as he shrugged his shoulders slightly. The offer was surely tempting and since Mike didn't have a place to stay, he decided to take the casino up on it.

"Okay, lead the way."

Mr. Sensor raised his right hand and motioned to someone in the distance behind Mike. As he turned to look in the same direction, two other employees arrived. One was a young, clean-cut man with short hair who appeared to be in his early twenties. He was dressed in blue slacks and burgundy sports jacket. The jacket was a tight fit to say the least, as his muscular build showed through. And Mike could tell he must be a bodyguard type. The other employee was a beautiful young female. Her dark flowing hair bounced playfully on her shoulders as she walked. She was dressed in a red blouse worn out of her skirt, which was dark blue. The skirt was very short and accentuated her long legs. As they arrived Mr. Sensor introduced them with the instructions to get Mike whatever he needed to make his stay comfortable. The female's name was Jennifer. When Mr. Sensor was finished, she turned to Mike and said, "Okay, Mr. Conners, here is a satchel for your winnings." Mike picked up the remaining chips and placed them in the carrier provided. He stood up and smiled his readiness to her.

"If you'll follow me, we need to go to the security office to get some information from you first."

"Information? What information?" Mike asked in a worried tone.

Jennifer stopped and looked at her fellow employee. Her eyes were squinting with the look of curiosity as to Mike's question. She looked back at Mike and in a calming way said, "Well, as you know, whenever anyone wins over a certain amount of money, we have to make a report for the Internal Revenue Service. And we give you a copy of a form, which then becomes your responsibility to report. It's no big deal, just your name, home address and social security number."

Mike didn't want to appear like he was hiding something, but knowing he didn't know his home address or social security number was going to be a problem. Plus he didn't have any sort of identification on him. He decided to just keep quiet and see how far he could go.

They arrived at the office door and Jennifer stuck a card in a reader to unlock it. They entered and walked over to a desk surrounded by several chairs.

"Sit here, Mr. Conners," Jennifer said. She then moved behind the desk and sat down at what appeared to be a computer terminal. While she was pressing assorted keys to set things up Mike couldn't help but notice the décor of the room. It was more like a private hotel room than an office, with lush carpeting, couches, large back chairs and heavy drapes on the windows. A large screen television mounted on the far wall was playing a movie. The male employee, who did not introduce himself, asked, "Would you like a cup of coffee or some other refreshment?"

Mike shifted slightly in his chair to answer him. "Oh, no thanks, I'm good." As he did this, he couldn't help but notice the camera which was mounted above the door that they had entered through. Mike looked at it and then back at the man and said, "Boy, they like to keep an eye on everything here, huh." The man didn't answer but smiled slightly and nodded in agreement.

"Okay, Mr. Conners. First name is Michael, correct?" Jennifer asked.

"That's correct."

"And your home address?"

Mike had thought about what questions were to be asked while they walked to the office and was ready.

"1561 Rowlandson Court." He spelled out the address to her as he somehow thought it would seem more believable.

"City?" she asked.

"Youngstown, Ohio," came his reply.

She snapped a look up from the keyboard with a big smile on her face.

"You're kidding; I lived in Youngstown for five years while I attended college there."

"Wow, small world," Mike said, trying to act as though he was happy to see someone from his hometown, a place he had no idea if he had ever visited. He couldn't help but think, *Shit, what are the odds of this?* The name came to him from an article he had read while at the hospital.

"How long have you lived there?" she asked.

Mike realized he had to keep the conversation flowing in a way that didn't arouse suspicion.

"Just a few months. I moved there from Orlando."

"Florida!" came a voice from behind Mike, who was startled by what he was afraid would be another challenge to his storytelling.

Mike half-turned and as he did, he managed to squeak out, "Yeah."

"I grew up in Orlando, great city to live in, but too many tourists. My folks still live there."

Mike didn't want to appear rude, but at the same time he didn't want to dig himself in too deep and get caught in a lie.

"Well, to tell you the truth, I really didn't like it there. Too many damn insects." He tried to sound annoyed in the hopes that it would shut off the many questions that he was afraid would follow if he allowed it.

"Yeah, I guess you're right, but if you think it's bad there, you should try Tampa. The mosquitoes there are like little jet dive bombers."

Mike twitched in his chair and let out a small puff of air before speaking. "Okay, what's next?"

Jennifer sensed his impatience and continued.

"Just your social security number."

Mike made up a nine-digit number that he hoped sounded believable. She didn't respond to his answer as she typed the information into the terminal but then asked him, "Do you have your driver's license on you?"

Mike momentarily patted his rear pocket area and at the same time said, "No, I'm sorry. I left everything at the place I'm staying." She looked at him as if to question his reply and then said, "Hmm, that might be a problem as far as issuing you a check for your winnings. You see ever since 9/11 the casinos have been very careful about it. I guess they're afraid of giving checks with their names on it to people without proof of who they are."

Mike was somewhat relieved, as he knew he would never be able to cash a check without identification, which he didn't have anyway.

"I understand. I think I would just rather, if it's OK with you, have the cash anyway."

"That's fine. If you want we can hold any amount you wish in our safe until you need it," she said.

Mike emptied the chips out on to the desk and counted his winnings. The final tally was $25,300. As he counted it, he couldn't help but feel nervous and his hands perspired with excitement.

"I'll take five thousand with me now and get more as I need it."

"Fifties and one-hundreds OK?" she asked.

He nodded approval.

Mike signed a receipt for his winnings and the form for the IRS and waited as Jennifer left the room with the chips to change them in. Mike remained in his chair and tried not to look at the male employee who was still standing in the same spot by the door. As he waited, the movie ended and a commercial about the Excalibur began playing. The announcer was explaining the benefits and amenities of the casino and how to gamble in Vegas.

"I guess you don't need any gaming tips," the male employee said with a little laugh. Mike didn't look at him and continued to stare at the screen.

"I remember when I first got here, boy, I thought it was amazing how much money people won and lost in one siting."

Mike still didn't move but felt the employee's eyes on him. "Mr. Conners?" he continued.

Mike knew he couldn't ignore him any longer and turned to reply. "Oh, yeah. I was pretty lucky that's all."

"I'll say. Boy if I didn't know better, I'd think you found some kind of system or something."

Mike didn't know how to reply to this and the tone of the man's voice made Mike a little uncomfortable.

"Well, if there was ever a system, I could probably sell it and make millions," Mike said as he turned back to the television, trying to act nonchalant about the whole thing.

"I'd be the first on my block to buy it."

Mike was about to answer him when Jennifer came back in.

"OK, Mr. Conners, here we go," she said as she stopped in front of the desk and counted out five thousand dollars in fifties and one-hundreds. She then took a small satchel from the desk drawer and gave it to him.

"Here, this is to keep it in if you so desire. Also here is a key card with your social security number assigned to it. You'll need it to retrieve the rest of your winnings when you're ready. Just present it to any cashier in the casino and they'll instruct you on how to get at the rest of your money. Don't lose it because without it, you'll have to prove who you are to get at your money. It can be embarrassing not to mention time-consuming."

"Thank you," Mike said.

"Now also will you be staying with us for a while?" she continued.

"Yes, I think Mr. Sensor said he would comp me a three-day stay."

"Very well."

She picked a phone and gave some instructions to the person on the other end. Just as she was hanging up another man dressed in a red blazer and blue slacks came in. Jennifer stood and introduced him as Remy, the concierge who would escort Mike to his room.

"Thanks again for all your help," Mike said as he got up and extended his hand to her.

"My pleasure and good luck to you, Mr. Conners."

Mike followed the concierge out of the room and down the hall to an elevator. Neither one of them spoke until they were inside and traveling down to the twenty-second floor.

Mike stood about three feet from and slightly to the rear of Remy, observing his appearance. Aside from his attire, he looked to be in his mid-forties and had a most peculiar and familiar fragrance about him. Mike was about to ask him what kind of cologne he was wearing, but decided that would sound strange and dismissed it. They reached their destination and Remy opened the door to Mike's room. The interior was dark as they walked inside and so Mike stood motionless waiting for his eyes to adjust. Just as he could start to make out the furnishings, the concierge opened the drapes. A flood of light from the afternoon sun filled the room, and Mike found himself squinting to readjust as he walked to the balcony, where a beautiful view of the city awaited him.

"The view from here is nicest in the early evening," Remy said.

"It's beautiful now!" Mike added. Mike turned and admired the room. It was quite large, with a king-size bed adorned in crimson colored drapes. It had thick carpeting with a medieval theme that was accented throughout.

Remy motioned to a nightstand by the bed and explained the phone system for making calls or getting assistance.

"If there is anything else you need, just ask," Remy said as he stood there momentarily as if waiting further instructions.

Mike looked at him and realized what he should do.

"Thanks for your help," Mike said as he gave the man a twenty.

Remy nodded and left the room.

Mike walked over to the bed, sat down and let out a large sigh of relief. He kicked off his sneakers and bounced once or twice as if to get a feel for the mattress before flinging himself backwards, coming to rest in the middle. He clasped his hands behind his neck and stared up at the ceiling.

Wow, this is incredible, he thought. He smiled slightly as he thought of the events up to this point. For the first time in a long time he felt that he had some control over his fate. A control that would help him discover who he was and what had happened to him. His thoughts took him back to the crap table and what he accomplished there. A new excitement began to take hold and feelings of doubt. He tried to dismiss them and decided to try watching television. He scanned the room for the remote and finally discovered it was on the nightstand just out of his reach. He stretched out his arm as far as it could go, but was still a foot short. Just as he was about to get up and reposition himself to reach it, the remote suddenly took off from its resting place and into Mike's hand. Mike's instinctively tightened his grip to take hold of it, and then just as quickly released his grip and threw the remote on the bed.

"Holy shit!" Mike lightly shouted.

He sat straight up on the bed and stared down at the remote. He glanced from there to his hands and back again. A feeling of amazement took hold as he tried to make sense of this. He found himself looking around the room as if to see if anyone was watching him. He edged backwards away from the remote to the far corner of the bed. He tried to concentrate on it as if to will it to come to him. After about five seconds he was about to give up when, all of a sudden, it started to move. Slowly at first and then just as before, it took off and landed square in his grip. Mike sat and stared at his hand clutching the remote. A small smile crept across his face and a weird giddy feeling overcame him. The smile grew to a small giggle and then to gut-jolting, uncontrollable laughter. Mike flung himself forward on his stomach still clutching the remote and waited for his feelings to subside.

This is incredible, he thought as he found himself shaking his head in denial of what he just witnessed. His thoughts brought him back to the hospital and the events there, especially the incident with Agent Martin. He then realized that in his attempt to protect himself, he caused the agent and the furniture in the hallway to act the way it did.

Mike got up off the bed and began pacing around the room, thinking of the other strange things that occurred since his rescue from the desert. He tried without success to remember his time there and try to recall how he came to be there. He found himself becoming angry at his failure to know the past. His only link that he felt sure of was his understanding of computers and the software that runs them. As he passed in front of a large mirror, which was also the door to the bathroom, his reflection made him stop. He looked himself up and down and turned from side to side in an attempt to see something that would help him remember more about himself or his past. He noticed that there was something about the way he was dressed that didn't feel just right. Walking over to a magazine rack near the bed, he picked one up. The cover read, "The Vegas Man, Then and Now." A photo of a well-dressed man with a modern double-breasted suit was seen looking into a mirror. The reflection was of the same man, but dressed in a suit from a bygone era. In looking at both the man and his reflection, Mike couldn't help but notice how different each one seemed. The old adage, "The clothes make the man" came to mind. It was then that the idea of getting new clothes hit him. He decided it was time to go shopping. Throwing the magazine on the bed, Mike left.

Chapter 12

Agent Grant sat at the table of the Starcrest Restaurant sipping a Pepsi through a straw while going over notes he had scratched out on a legal pad. A grilled cheese sandwich lay half-eaten on his plate. Picking it up he tore off bite-sized pieces and stuck them in his mouth. He was almost finished when his cell phone went off.

"Hello."

"Hi, Phil, it's Bob. I have some info for you."

"I'm listening."

"First off, the partial that we lifted from the hospital room came back as inconclusive. Not enough points to make a definite ID."

"Terrific. What else."

"I started looking at the phone logs from yesterday forward for the doctor. I didn't see anything out of the ordinary except one thing. He received a phone call from a pay phone at the Excalibur. It lasted about five minutes, so I don't think it was a wrong number."

"Good. What do you say we take Mr. Conners' photo and pay the place a visit?"

"I'll meet you in the front lobby," Phil said.

The two agents disconnected and within ten minutes, Agent Grant was pulling into the parking area for the casino. He put on his sports jacket but left off his tie. Walking into the lobby, he saw Bob Durham standing in front of a slot machine feeding it nickels at a rather fast rate.

"You could at least play the quarter machines," Phil said.

Bob looked up startled by the remark, laughed and said, "On our salary, I don't think so."

Agent Grant gave Bob a photo and said, "Let's get started before I decide to join you."

A small grunt came from Bob, who added, "Spoil sport."

The two agents walked up to the front desk.

"Excuse me, sir, I'm Agent Grant, Federal Bureau of Investigation," Phil said as he displayed his credentials to the young man behind the mahogany counter. Before he could continue, the man reached for a phone and was advising the person on the other end of Agent Grant's presence. Phil waited for him to finish and then continued.

"I'd like to know if you have a man staying here that might have registered under the name of Mike Conners?" Phil showed the photo to the clerk.

The hotel employee glanced at it without touching it.

"I'm sorry, I don't know if I can give you that information without permission."

"What do you mean?"

"Well, you see, I'm new here and we have strict regulations pertaining to the privacy of our guests. I just called for my supervisor to assist you. Anyway, I just got on duty ten minutes ago and I don't recognize the man."

Phil pursed his lips twice and then noticed another employee about five feet to his left. The second employee was staring at the first employee with a look of concern. When the first employee noticed his stare, he turned to Phil and added, "He just got on duty also. The previous shift has already left for the day. If I do see him though, I'll notify my supervisor for you. See, we're not allowed to comment on our guests directly without notifying someone."

Phil couldn't help but feel slightly annoyed at his response to the question.

"Well, could you at least look to see if he's registered?"

The clerk wrinkled his nose and brow and looked at the agent as if he was waiting to be punished. "Are you a relative of this guest?"

"No, I'm not."

"Then I'm sorry, but I need permission," he said as he backed up slightly.

"Terrific. I'll bet you never do anything without asking permission," Phil said sarcastically.

The hotel employee didn't respond to Phil's statement and continued to glance nervously at his fellow employee who now was busy with a hotel guest.

"Which way to the security office?" Phil said

Before the man could answer the agent, a voice came from Phil's right.

"May I help you?"

Phil turned to see a tall man with short-cropped hair dressed in a blue business suit stop and look at both the agents.

"My name is Jeff Jarman. I'm head of security for the hotel."

Phil produced his identification for the man to see. "I'm Phil Grant and this is Agent Durham, Federal Bureau of Investigation."

Mr. Jarman looked at the ID and then at both of the agents again. As he did Phil continued. "We're here trying to locate a subject who we feel might be staying here at the casino."

"First things first, Agent Grant. What office are the two of you from?"

"Chicago. Why?"

"Well, to be quite honest with you, I like to check just to make sure you are who you say you are. After all it's very easy to make a fake ID these days."

Mr. Jarman picked up a phone from the desk and requested the person on the other end to verify the information given. He hung up and turned toward the agents and asked, "OK, what's his name?"

"He probably will be using the name Mike Conners."

"Is he wanted for a crime or a fugitive, or someone we should be worried about?" asked Mr. Jarman.

"No, nothing like that. We just need to ask him some questions in reference to a case we are working on. We got a tip he might be staying here."

"Well, if he's not a wanted person or a security risk, we really don't like to bother our guests if it isn't necessary."

Agent Grant looked at Bob, who could see his partner's frustration level rising. Bob decided that maybe they should make it necessary.

"Look, Mr. Jarman, we don't want to make it sound necessary, but if you like, we could arrange for it to be."

Jeff looked at Agent Durham and didn't quite know how to take the agent's statement.

"We're just looking for some cooperation here," Bob added. Mr. Jarman eyed the other employees behind the counter before responding.

"Alright," he said as he moved to an area behind the counter to face a computer terminal. His fingers began playing with the keyboard as his eyes focused on the screen.

Phil produced the photo of Mike Conners and let the security officer take a long look.

Mr. Jarman briefly looked at the photo and then at the screen again. He took a slow deep breath as he waited for the information to appear. Before it did, the attendant standing next to him started waving a telephone receiver in front of his face.

"Excuse me, Mr. Jarman, this is for you."

Jeff Jarman looking slightly annoyed at the way the employee got his attention and he appeared to make a mental note to speak to him about it later. As he spoke, he turned away from the agents to listen before responding.

"Okay, thanks," he said and hung up. Turning once again to face the agents he continued. "Well, it seems the two of you are legit."

Phil looked at Bob who was smirking and grunting at the same time. He could tell by his look that he was probably thinking *No shit.*

"That was fast," Phil said. "Now can we get on with it?"

Mr. Jarman again turned his attention to the terminal and then said, "Ahh, yeah." He said this as if he were talking directly to the computer terminal.

"Is that a yes?" Phil asked.

"Well, to be quite honest with you, we do have a subject staying here as a comp guest using that name."

"Comp guest, you mean, he's staying here for free?" Bob asked.

"Well, yes." Mr. Jarman hesitated. "There are special circumstances that would allow that to happen. I think we should take a walk to the office and see if anyone else can help. Anyway if this is the man you're interested in, I need to stop by there to get a security key card for the room."

"That would be great," Phil said.

The two agents followed Mr. Jarman to a hallway where eight elevator doors, four on each side, stood awaiting the guests. They stood in silence facing the doors on the right side of the hallway. One finally opened and the three men entered for the ride to the twenty-fifth floor. As their door closed, another on the left side of the hall opened. Mike Conners calmly walked out on his way to what he thought would be a nice shopping spree for some new clothes.

Chapter 13

Mike walked through the casino area on his way to the shops. He decided to try the stores in the hotel first. He remembered seeing a clothing shop called Marshall-Rousso located on the second level. As he walked, he passed a restaurant called The Steakhouse at Camelot. The odor of the food was too much to resist, so he detoured to satisfy his hunger. As he entered he was approached by a well-dressed man who asked him if he was dining alone. Mike told him he was, and was taken to a small table near the back of the restaurant. Mike felt comfortable here and the way he was seated gave him a good view of the main floor and entranceway. He sat for several minutes examining the menu and sipping on the water in front of him. He decided on the house steak with salad and baked potato. Placing the menu on the table and looking around for his waiter, he noticed him at a table that was about thirty feet from his. He seemed to be involved in a lively one-sided discussion with the guest there, a middle-aged man with combed-back hair and a rugged, pockmarked face. Mike suddenly recognized him as the same man that was at the crap tables. Mike couldn't make out the words but could tell by the waiter's demeanor and stance that it wasn't a pleasant conversation. The guest was seemingly belittling the waiter for some unknown reason. It was obvious that the waiter was intimidated and suddenly walked away and disappeared through two double doors to the kitchen area. About three minutes later, the waiter reappeared with another man who was carrying a tray of food. The two of them returned to the man's table and a few words were exchanged before the food was placed on the table. Mike got the waiter's attention as he turned and then noticed that the man was now staring in his direction. The waiter approached Mike and said, "I'm sorry for the delay in service' sir, are you ready to order?"

"Ah yeah, sure, I'll have the house steak with a baked potato. I'd also like to have Italian dressing on the salad."

"And to drink?"

"Just a Sprite or 7-Up."

"Very well. I'll get your order right in"

The waiter turned and left. Mike saw him stop momentarily again at the man's table and as the waiter spoke, Mike noticed that the man said something and as he did, he pointed briefly in Mike's direction. Mike began to feel a little uneasy about this, but tried not to show it. He picked up the wine list from the table and pretended to be reading it. About three minutes passed before the waiter again appeared and brought Mike his drink. As he placed it down, Mike couldn't contain his curiosity any longer and asked, "What was the matter with that gentleman at the other table?"

"Oh, he's just one of those people who is hard to please." Mike noticed a sudden change in the waiter's face. "By the way, you don't by any chance know him do you?" the waiter said with a look of concern.

"No, no, I don't. And even if I did, it wouldn't matter."

The waiter seemed relieved and added, "We try to be very accommodating to all our guests, no matter how they feel."

The two men smiled briefly at each other and then the waiter turned his attention to other guests. Mike placed the wine list back in its holder and began looking around the room admiring the décor and trying to see what other guests were eating. The room was dimly lit and so it was hard to distinguish exact meals. Several televisions were strategically placed around the dining area for guests to view different sporting events as they ate. Mike found one almost directly in front of him which featured horse racing and began watching it. After several minutes, he became bored with it and began looking around for another set to view. When his gaze came to the area where the man was eating, he noticed that he was talking on a cell phone. Mike didn't think much of this until he noticed that as he talked he kept glancing in Mike's direction. An uneasy feeling again rose up from within and Mike found himself shifting his position while looking away. Mike decided to once again ignore his feelings and not make anything out of the looks he was getting. He tried to reassure himself that he was only overreacting. There was a television on the far wall and Mike stared at it trying to concentrate on the content of the show.

It looked like a group of people were whitewater rafting and one of them had fallen in. The others had formed a circle around their comrade and were trying to get him on board one of the rafts. The person in the water kept disappearing beneath the rapids and then reappearing momentarily, flying up out of the water before being dragged under again. This lasted about three minutes and it looked like the person in the water was getting beat up pretty bad by the rocks. On one of the rafters jumped out from under the water; he managed to land on the edge of one of the rafts. Two of the passengers in the raft dragged him on board to safety. The cameras zoomed in for a close-up of the man's injuries. As the fellow rafters attended to him, blood could be seen coming from his forehead.

Wow. I guess he won't be doing that too much, Mike thought. His concentration was broken by the arrival of his food. As Mike looked at the waiter placing the meal in front of him, he couldn't help but glance in the direction of the man who had been staring at him. He was gone.

"I guess you're happy our friend left," Mike said as the waiter arranged the food before him. The waiter stopped momentarily to glance over before replying.

"Oh, I didn't even notice. I guess Mr. Prescott had his fill."

Right after he said this, he realized that he should not have mentioned the man's name to another guest, as it was not exactly the professional thing to do. The waiter abruptly stood straight and excused himself and left Mike to his meal. Mike was almost finished when his waiter appeared before him and asked if he wanted dessert.

"No, I think I've had enough."

"Very well, sir, I'll be right back with your check."

Mike paid for his meal and left a twenty-dollar tip.

Chapter 14

The cab pulled up to the front of the Excalibur and stopped.

"Okay, ma'am, here we are," said the driver. He turned in his seat and looked at Melissa Conners, who was fumbling in her pocketbook for money.

"I'll get your bags for you," he continued with a big smile on his face as he hit the trunk release. Getting out of the cab and sauntering around to the rear, he caught the trunk lid as it bounced open. He struggled slightly, taking the two large leather suitcases out, and placed them on a cart that was stationed curbside for the hotel guests. An attendant for the hotel was right there awaiting Melissa as she got out of the vehicle.

"Wow, it's warmer than I thought," she said as she pulled her long blond hair back and up off her shoulders.

"Actually it's not bad; usually it's about ten degrees hotter," the attendant said.

She was wearing a yellow pants suit with a matching button-down blouse. Her jacket hung over her left arm, which also supported her pocketbook. In her right hand she held a hundred-dollar bill and extended it to the cab driver.

"I'm sorry but I don't have anything smaller," she said with a smile that would melt most men. The cab driver looked at the hotel attendant who intervened.

"I can make change for you." He reached into his pocket and produced a wad of bills and switched Melissa's for twenties.

After settling her fare with the driver she turned to see the attendant waiting with his hand on the suitcase cart. Actually he was staring at Melissa in a way that made her feel a little uncomfortable.

"Hi, my name is Tony," he said as he extended his hand to shake hers. She thought it was a little odd for an attendant to introduce himself, but then dismissed it.

"Hi, I'm Melissa Conners," she said as she quickly withdrew her hand and tried not to look him in the eye. She had learned a long time ago that it was not always good to be too friendly or encourage interest by looking too long at a person.

He looked to be in his mid-twenties with thick, wavy, black hair and a dark complexion. Melissa thought him to be Italian.

"I'll take these for you. Just follow me," he said.

Melissa hesitated to allow him to get in front of her. As they walked in through the doors of the hotel, the attendant made the customary small talk.

"Is this your first time with us?"

"Yes, it is. I've been to Vegas before but never stayed here."

The attendant gave her a look as if he were trying figure out if her remark was made in a good or bad way.

Melissa noticed and added, "I figured I'd try someplace different. Castles have always intrigued me anyway."

The attendant looked her up and down, smiled and said, "I'm sure you'll enjoy yourself. Are you here alone?"

Melissa found herself briefly wondering about this and decided to lie. "No, my husband's on his way."

"Great; the two of you will have fun I'm sure," he said with a hint of sarcasm as he accented the word two.

Melissa found his remark annoying but decided to just ignore it.

They reached the front desk and the attendant parked the cart next to it. He momentarily stood there with Melissa as if waiting to be recognized by the person behind the counter. Melissa took this to mean that he was awaiting a tip.

She gave him a five and said, "Thank you."

"You're welcome, have a nice day," he said and then turned to the receptionist behind the counter and said, "This is Mrs. Conners. She will be checking in. Her husband is to follow shortly."

As he said this he smiled briefly and looked at Melissa with a look that told her he didn't believe her. She remained poker-faced as he walked away.

As she waited to be checked in she thought about her remark to the attendant. She was not sure what made her say this. She wasn't even sure why she picked the Excalibur. She thought of how nice it would be if it were true. She missed Mike terribly and nothing would have made her happier than if they could be together again. She knew she was wrong to take off and leave the protection of the safe house, but she felt if she didn't do something, she would go nuts. She would give herself two weeks before notifying the FBI that she was safe and then she would return to the house. She didn't care about the consequences she could face. She had been alone four months and was beginning to feel that she would never see Mike again. She also felt that the FBI was not always truthful about Mike's whereabouts.

"Good afternoon. May I help you?" the lady behind the reception counter said.

"Yes, I'd like a room for a few nights."

"Just the two of you?"

Melissa stood there momentarily assessing this question.

"Ah, yes, just the two of us."

"A few nights, OK, we have packages to save money if you book a room for five nights."

Melissa thought about this for a second before agreeing. Her package included three shows and three dinners. "If something comes up and I decide to leave early, is there an extra fee?"

"Not as long as you give twelve hours' notice," she said

Melissa thought this to be a little odd but accepted anyway.

The receptionist finished with Melissa's check in and gave her two credit card keys.

"You're in room 1836 in the north tower. This is Tom; he will take your luggage up to your room for you. If you need anything just pick up the phone. Enjoy your stay."

"Thank you," she said as she finished signing her receipt.

"Hi, shall I show you to your room?"

"No, thanks; I'm going to take a look around a bit before I go up," she said.

"Very well then, your luggage will be waiting when you get there."

The bellhop transferred the bags to another cart as Melissa watched. She then turned once again to the desk clerk and asked, "Do you have a map of the hotel?"

"Sure, here you go," she said as she placed it on the counter in front of Melissa.

Picking it up she went to a small couch on the other side of the room sat down and started glancing at it. The map had a basic floor plan of the hotel and casino. As she sat there studying it she became aware of small bar off to her right. There were several people sitting there watching a television behind the bar. One of them seemed to be staring at her. He was a man in his forties with a rugged complexion. He was talking on a cell phone and when he realized Melissa was looking at him he suddenly looked away. Melissa didn't know why, but there was something about the man that made her feel uncomfortable. She decided it was time to go up to her room.

Lance Prescott sat on the bar stool. He held a drink in one hand and his cell phone in the other. His talked in short phrases.

"I don't fuckin' believe this. I mean I'm gonna do some checking."

He paused to hear the subject on the other end before continuing. "Yeah, I mean I've seen them both. The only strange thing was they weren't together. In fact I saw him a day before I saw her. Maybe they don't want to bring attention to themselves. I'll find out and get back to you." He placed the phone in his pocket and watched Melissa get up from the couch and walk towards the elevator. He waited until she was out of sight before moving. Walking up to the check-in desk he stood there trying to act lost.

"May I help you sir?"

"Ah, yes, I hope so. I was supposed to meet my wife in the lobby but I kind of got caught up in the casino." He paused to act embarrassed. "Did a Mrs. Conners check in yet?"

"Oh, you mean Melissa Conners?"

"Yes, that's her; did I miss her by much?"

"No, in fact I believe she just went up to your room."

"Maybe if I hurry, I can meet her just as she arrives," he said now moving as if it was real important not to keep her waiting. He turned away and then back nervously before the attendant could react to other people in line.

"Oh, wait, I guess it would help if I knew what room we were staying in."

The attendant smiled and said, "Room 1836; that would be in the north tower."

Lance gave a sigh of relief. "Thank you."

He walked briskly toward the elevator and waited until he was inside before relaxing his posture. There was no one inside with him and a second later he was back on the phone.

"Jim, hi, it's me again."

"What did you find out?" the man on the other end said.

"I was right, that's what. I mean at first I wasn't sure, as they weren't together and didn't even check in together. I generally never forget a beautiful face. The receptionist at the front desk just confirmed it."

Lance paused to allow the man on the other end to respond.

"That's great; Mr. Swindell is going to be happy to hear it. I'll notify him and get back to you. Even though I'm positive what he's gonna want to do."

"Okay, let me know as quick as you can as I don't know how long they're going to be here."

Lance placed the cell back in his pocket just as the door to the elevator opened on the eighteenth floor. He walked out and glanced in both directions before deciding to go right. The hallway was empty except for one bellhop who was standing near a door writing down something on a piece of paper. As Lance approached him the man looked up to greet him.

"Good day, sir."

"Hi," Lance said as he looked at the number 1836 on the door.

"Can I help you?"

"Ah, no thanks," Lance replied and then kept on walking to the end and made a left.

Melissa arrived at her room to find her luggage neatly placed on the floor just inside the door. She glanced around and inspected the accommodations which met her approval. She walked over to a table by the window and sat down to inspect the map she had received from the front desk. She wanted to plan out her day. Looking out to see the other towers with the mountains rising up in the distance, he found the view to be both impressive and relaxing. She thought about ordering some food from room service but decided that it would be much better to get out and go exploring. After all, that's why she left the confines of her safe house. She had enough solitary to last her for a while. She unpacked her clothes, showered and then sat on the bed to watch some TV while she dried her hair. Twenty minutes later she felt ready to leave and experience what the brochure claims would be fun, twenty-four hours a day.

She arrived at the casino at the same time that Lance Prescott was ending his third conversation of the day with his connection from Chicago. He stood there with another associate and watched her stop by one of the many change makers that roam the casino floor. They watched as she exchanged bills for rolls of quarters and proceeded to the video poker machines.

Which one, which one, Melissa thought as she stood there juggling rolls of quarters between her hands.

"You'll never win if you don't play," came a voice from to her right. Melissa turned to see a man walk past her and sit at the last machine in the row. He smiled at her and continued. "I couldn't help notice you standing there."

Melissa smiled back. "I like to get a feel for the machine before I waste my money on it," she said.

"I used to do the same thing, and then I read this book on tips for winning at slots."

Melissa's as a rule didn't like conversations with strangers that extended past the usual pleasantries associated with greetings or comments on trivial things. She had reason to be especially cautious of late, given her decision to take a vacation without permission. There was something she found pleasant in his voice and her curiosity about his statement piqued her interest.

"Have a seat," he said as he pointed to the machine next to his. Melissa hesitated as she glanced around and then sat down.

She noticed that he didn't look at her at first and seemed to be studying the machine. She found this seemingly lack of interest in her relaxing.

"You see, casinos are here to make money. They have become very sophisticated in their marketing techniques. They know how to lure people in to spending money at their establishments."

He turned to her and smiled, making sure she was listening before looking back at his machine. Melissa not only was listening but also was trying to figure this guy out. He was very attractive; she figured him to be in his late thirties. His clean looks and well-manicured hands along with the way he talked and carried himself suggested he might be some kind of professional. The big question was, professional what? She picked up a bucket next to her machine and placed her coins in it as she listened further.

"Everything that a casino does is camouflaged to make it look like it's for your benefit and enjoyment. And to some extent it is, but the main reasoning behind it is to make money."

Melissa thought about it for a second and found herself subconsciously nodding agreement. He glanced at her again and smiled. He was happy she agreed as it told him he was getting somewhere.

He figured he should disarm her some more and extended his hand to her.

"Oh, by the way, I'm Adam. Adam Sheppard."

As their hands came together she could feel his warmth and strength.

"I'm Melissa."

She withdrew and found herself blush slightly. She felt uncomfortable with the way he made her feel. Before she could react he continued. "In this book I read, it explained that the sights and sounds of a casino are all there to lure you in. If you can look at the way they market it then you have a better chance at winning."

Melissa wasn't quite sure what he meant by this and was hoping he would qualify it.

"Let's take the slot machines for example."

He said this as he started to place quarters in and press the button to start the action.

"Did you ever notice the rhythmic sound of all the slot machines and the ding-ding-ding noise that they make?

"Yes," Melissa said as she glanced around the casino and found herself listening for it.

"Studies have been done that show that certain repetitive frequencies have a habitual effect on the brain. They become somewhat habit-forming and soothing. Sort of like a mantra that a yogi might use."

Melissa smiled slightly as what he said kind of made sense to her.

"Yeah, I see what you mean. It sort of lulls you in."

"The casinos know that the more you hear this, the more you're likely to come back just for that sound alone."

He glanced at her again before continuing. "It doesn't stop there though. The colors and the lighting are also there to make you feel comfortable and confident."

"Which of course would make one stay longer," she added.

"Exactly," he said as he made certain he smiled at her and their eyes met a little longer than the first time. He could tell she was becoming more comfortable with him.

"Now if you stay long enough in a casino and observe the

people playing the slots, you'll begin to notice that certain machines pay out more than others. These machines are strategically placed in certain areas of the casino to attract customers to play there. The trick is to be observant and find these machines. A lot of times though they are placed at the end of a row of machines so that people who hear a winning machine are attracted to that area and then just funnel down the row to try their luck at one of those machines."

Melissa thought about what Adam said and was about to comment on that when his machine began ringing with the unmistakable sound that told others he had hit. A look of surprise and happiness spread across her face. Adam turned to her and smiled back.

"See, I told you, nothing to it," he said.

"Wow, I guess you're right," she added.

It wasn't a big win for Adam, but it was enough to help him gain more of Melissa's trust.

The two talked for a while longer and Melissa found herself becoming more and more at ease with him. She had begun playing at her machine and the two kept their talk light and non-personal. It wasn't long before she had run out of coins.

"I guess this machine is not a winner," she said.

Adam looked at her and then pointed to an area on the other side of the casino.

"The progressive slots are over there. They have a little bit better pay-out with more options."

"Oh, great, you mean they have more ways to lose your money." Melissa giggled slightly as she said this just to let him know she wasn't bothered by the prospect of losing.

The two got up and began to walk in the direction of the progressive slots. Adam pointed the way and allowed Melissa to take the lead. As they passed where Lance Prescott was still standing, Adam glanced his way and winked to let his associate know progress was moving along.

They had to pass an alcove area to get to the progressive slot machines. The alcove had a small bar and a waitress station from where the floor waitresses would pick up the drinks that were given freely to the customers while they were actively gambling.

As they got to the bar, Adam stopped to buy a drink.

"Can I get you something?"

Melissa stopped with his comment and turned to face the bar. The bartender looked at her and smiled.

"Ah, yeah sure, I'll have a strawberry daiquiri."

Adam sat at the bar to wait for their order. Melissa stood there momentarily looking around. A slight feeling of guilt rose up from within. She dismissed it and sat down.

Adam paid the bartender and as Melissa raised her glass to taste it, Adam offered a toast.

"May your winnings be big and your losses be small, a gambler's motto is winner take all!"

She smiled as he said it and for an instant as their eyes met, he could sense a slight uneasiness.

"I'm sorry; you know I don't mean to seem pretentious about my gambling abilities. At least I hope you don't think that. And I hope you don't think that I'm trying to pick you up or anything like that. I mean I don't even know if you're here by yourself or maybe married with kids, or anything. For all I know you could be a mass murderer running from the law." He chuckled with that before continuing. "It's just that I see so many people wasting their money not knowing about the huge advantage the casinos have over them. When I saw you walking around, I just felt that I should help you out."

Melissa swallowed and forced a smile at the same time. Placing her glass on the bar she said, "Well, thanks, but I don't feel like

I'm going to become their next victim. And no, I don't think you were trying to pick me up, and if I were here with someone, I would have mentioned it. It's just that I haven't been on vacation for so long. I guess I feel a little guilty about it." That's as far as Melissa would allow herself to reveal anything about how she came to the casino.

The two sat there enjoying their drinks and Adam continued to talk about ways of winning.

The moments turned to minutes and their talk moved onto other things. Adam told her that he was the vice president of a medical supply company in Phoenix and was divorced with no children. He would have liked to have had them but his wife's affair destroyed that along with their marriage. Melissa found herself feeling sorry for him, which is exactly what he wanted to help gain her trust. Before Melissa had realized it, a whole hour and three drinks had passed. She had let her guard down and discovered that it felt good to be able to talk to someone without having to be guarded as to what to say.

Adam was looking at Melissa and at the same time he was looking past her to Lance. Adam saw him look down at his watch and tap it several times. He knew this was a signal to hurry his advances along. He gave a return signal which told Lance to be patient and all was well.

"By the way, what is your favorite type of food?" Adam asked.

The question took Melissa by surprise and she wrinkled her brow as she thought.

"Ah, I'm partial to seafood."

Adam gave her a strange look, which made Melissa ask, "Why? Is that bad for people who gamble?"

"Oh, no, not at all, in fact people who consume seafood are probably better at gambling than others."

Adam tried to keep a straight face as he said this, but his slight smile gave him away.

"Oh, come on now! You can't be serious," she said.

His smile turned into a slight giggle as he looked down at the floor and then back up to her.

"Well, no, I'm just teasing. Actually I was getting a little hungry," Adam said with a smile. "Would you like to get something to eat?"

Melissa hadn't given much thought to food since she arrived on the casino floor. Even though she was feeling the effects of the drinks, Adams question made her realize she was indeed hungry.

"Ah, yeah, I think I should have something. I saw a nice little café around here somewhere, The Sherwood Forest Café I think it's called," she said.

Adam knew the place but he had to convince her to leave the hotel so he and Lance could put their plan into motion.

"I've been coming to Vegas for a lot of years, and I can definitely tell you that there are way better places than that. I know a real nice restaurant that serves the best seafood this side of the Mississippi. It's only about ten minutes from here."

"I don't know," she began and then stopped as he continued.

"It's on me. And I'll have you back in plenty of time to play as many slots as your heart desires."

Melissa smiled slightly and thought, *Why not?*

"Okay, Mr. Sheppard, I'll take you up on your offer, if you can promise me we'll be back in two hours." Melissa didn't know why she said this or needed to have a time limit, but it made her feel better.

Adam paid the bar tab and then took out his cell phone to call for a ride as the two of them walked toward the front exit of the hotel.

"You have your own car service?" Melissa asked.

"Adam smiled slightly and said, "I make arrangements every time I come to Vegas for a private driver. It makes getting around a whole lot easier."

His answer made Melissa wonder more about him. "How often do you come here?" she asked.

"Probably too much, not like it's an obsession or anything. A lot of times I just come to people-watch or take in a show. I used to come just for the gambling. Somewhere between the lost wages and the hangovers that you can so easily get here, it all evolved into something else."

Adam threw in this statement just for good measure. He knew he already had her convinced that he was an all-around good guy and he could tell she let her guard down enough for his plan to succeed.

Chapter 15

Agents Grant and Durham Followed Mr. Jarman out of the elevator and down a long hall to the security office. As they entered they noticed how plush and comfortable-looking everything was.

It appeared as just another hotel room only much bigger. There were several video monitors set up along the walls and desks manned with personnel in front of them. The men followed him through this room and into an adjoining one which was bigger than the first. Several offices connected to this room and some just appeared as glass lined cubicles. Jennifer Escolone sat in one of these. She looked up as the men entered. Jeff Jarman motioned for her to follow them into his office. She hung up her phone and proceeded to the office. As she entered, Mr. Jarman was already typing into a terminal at his desk.

"Miss Escalone, these are Agents Grant and Durham from the FBI," he said without looking away from the screen. As she shook their hands he continued. "Their interested in a guest we have staying here that I see you have listed with complimentary status."

As he said this Agent Grant produced a photo for her to view. "Oh, you mean Mr. Conners. Yes, an interesting gentleman, to say the least, and very lucky." She accented the word "very" and smiled as she spoke, but then quickly changed her expression when she noticed the serious looks on the agents face.

Jeff Jarman looked up from his terminal and said, "It seems Mr. Conners had a nice run at one of our crap tables and was rewarded with a free stay for three days."

"What's a nice run?" Phil asked.

"Normally if a customer is lucky and wins twenty thousand or more, we consider it a nice run. Mr. Conners won over twenty-five thousand."

"Great, I hope he doesn't decide to leave before we can talk to him. You can get pretty far on that," Bob said.

"Well, actually he only took five grand with him, the rest we're holding for him in our safe," Jennifer added.

Phil placed the photo back in his pocket and asked, "Well, can you take us to his room now?"

"I don't see why not. You say you just want to ask him some questions, right?" asked Mr. Jarman. The two agents looked at each other and decided it was time to let the security people know more.

"Well, actually we do just want to ask him some questions, but it's going to have to be at a different location," Phil said.

"You see one of our agents was assaulted, and Mr. Conners is a very strong suspect."

Jeff glanced at Jennifer and rolled his eyes before coming to rest on Phil.

"Why didn't you just tell me that from the beginning?"

"There are certain things, for security reasons, which I can't discuss with you, Mr. Jarman."

"Now you're making it seem like Mr. Conners is some kind of threat to my hotel."

"Like I told you before, he's not a security risk. It's just that this case we're working on is a little complicated. I need to take Mr. Conners in for questioning and then that should be the end of it for you."

Jeff Jarman took a security card out of his desk and placed it in a card reader connected to his terminal. After programming it with the code for Mike Conners' room, he stood up.

"Okay, then let me ring his room first to see if he is there."

"I don't think that's a good idea. I would rather just take a chance that he's in and worry about him not being there later," Phil said.

Jeff shrugged his shoulders and then turned to Jennifer. "You stay here and keep an eye on the monitors; if you should see Mr. Conners give me a shout."

Jennifer nodded that she understood and left the office. The two agents followed Jeff Jarman back to the elevators and proceeded down to the twenty-second floor. Three minutes later they were standing in front of the door to Mike's room. As Jeff took the key card out of his pocket, Phil placed his hand on his forearm and said, "Wait, Mr. Jarman, I think it would be a good idea if you let me go first."

Jeff hesitated momentarily before turning the card over to the agent and stepping back. Bob Durham flanked the entrance from the other side. They entered the room and made a quick assessment and were disappointed to find it empty. It was pretty clean; the only thing out of place was a magazine lying open on the bed.

"I was afraid of this," Bob said.

Bob looked at Mr. Jarman and then at Phil before adding, "I'll flip you for who stays."

Phil thought about this for a minute, recalling the events at the hospital before responding, "No, need to, we'll both stay."

As he said this he turned to Jeff and continued, "You don't mind, do you?"

"Not at all, and if we locate him somewhere in the casino, do you want my security people to hold him?"

"No, just let me know and we'll go to him. Here is my card with my cell number on it."

Jeff took the card and placed in his pocket and said, "If he shows up here first, just let me know when you're leaving with him so I can open the room up for others."

Phil shook his head in agreement as Mr. Jarman left and then moved to a seat near the window to make himself comfortable. Both agents knew it could be hours before Mike returned if at all. Bob Durham turned on the television and sat on the bed, and after about thirty seconds deciding that he didn't want to get to comfortable, he moved to a couch.

Chapter 16

Mike Conners, having satisfied his hunger, strolled out of the steakhouse at Camelot to continue his clothes shopping. He was on level two of the hotel which had mainly places to eat and so he decided to take the escalator down to the casino level and explore there. As he entered the casino floor and stepped off the escalator, a strange feeling came over him. He was walking on solid ground but he felt like he was still on the escalator. He stopped walking and looked around and tried to figure out what was going on. A young man was standing off in the distance. Mike couldn't help but notice that he appeared quite nervous and seemed as if he was waiting for something or somebody. As Mike got closer to him the feeling intensified. A few moments passed and then suddenly the feeling stopped. Mike was relieved it did, but then also noticed that the young man was gone too. Mike shook his head as if to clear it and decided to just chalk it up to the escalator and the steak meal he just consumed. He looked further for a place to shop but couldn't find any. He decided to just ask at the front desk for a good place to buy clothes. On his way there, he found himself again walking through the casino.

As he did, a large group of about twenty-five senior citizens was coming from the other direction on their way from the casino slot machines. Mike thought how happy they looked as they made their way to the bank of elevators behind him. The group was strolling along in loud conversation. One could see that they were enjoying their time spent there. A few of them were carrying buckets of quarters in one hand and drinks in the other. As Mike watched the feeling of uneasiness returned. He shook his head slightly and ran his hand through his hair as if to get it out of his face. He was looking directly into the group and suddenly noticed that there was some kind of commotion that was separating them. Heads and bodies seemed to be violently pushed apart. He stopped his forward movement to get a better look at what was going on. Just as he did, the same young man who Mike first noticed when he got off the escalator burst into view form the center of the group. He was running at full speed in Mike's direction. He had two buckets of coins grasped tightly in his arms and wore a panicked look like that of a zebra trying to get away from a hungry lion on the African planes. The crescendo of voices from the senior citizens quickly got the attention of other people on the casino floor.

"Stop thief!" and "Somebody grab him!" could be heard coming from the group. The young man had obviously grabbed the buckets from members of the group and was attempting to make his get-away. He was about twenty feet from Mike and two security personnel were converging from two different directions. Mike didn't have time to move out of the way and quickly put his hands up in front of his chest, closed his eyes and braced for what he thought would be a sure sudden impact. In the brief seconds that followed and before Mike could open his eyes, Mike heard what sounded like hundreds of coins being dropped on the floor. It was at that moment that he opened his eyes to see the young man sprawled out on the floor about ten feet from him, and the coins from the two buckets still flying around and bouncing every which way. The security people were on him and some of the senior citizens could be seen clapping their approval for a good job done by the security people in catching him. Mike walked slowly past the capture and could hear the conversation between the young man and security duo.

"What the hell happened?" the now dazed young man asked.

The two security people looked at him and at each other with questions of their own.

"How the hell do we know, buddy? What made you decide to throw the coins in the air like that?" one of them asked.

The other added, "I guess you thought it would help you escape, huh."

The young man still shaken by the experience, looked directly at Mike. "That man pushed me."

The bigger of the two men just looked at the young man and then briefly at Mike and said, "You're crazy. I saw the whole thing, he didn't even touch you."

Not wanting to attract any more attention, Mike tried to walk away as fast as he could.

"Hold up a second, sir," one of the security guards said. Mike tried to act as if he didn't hear him.

"Sir!" he said a bit louder.

Mike stopped in his tracks, sighed, and then turned to face the man, who by now was standing right next to him.

"Yes?" Mike said.

"Hi, my name is Don. I'm with hotel security. I know you must have seen this guy running toward you. Did you by any chance try to stop him?"

Mike had a worried look on his face as he answered, "Why no, not at all. I mean sure, I saw him running, and I thought he was gonna run right into me, but I never touched him."

"I didn't think so, but I had to ask anyway to cover ourselves in case of pending law suits."

"I understand. No problem."

By now the crowd of senior citizens had caught up and one of them, a small frail-looking women with glasses too big for her face said, "Thank you so much for stopping this rude young man. He almost got away with my winnings, but because of your quick response, I can continue my enjoyment at the casino." As she said this she reached into her pocketbook and attempted to give one of the security men a handful of quarters from it.

Before she could reach out her hand, another woman standing next to her stopped her. "Now, Janice, I don't think that will be necessary. The man was only doing his job, and besides, I think that other man over there might have had something to do with capturing the thief. From where I stood, it looked like he might have pushed him or something. I mean, I saw his hand go up and then I saw the young man who took your winnings go down on the floor."

"Oh my, then maybe I should be thanking him." As she said this, a small murmur of agreement could be heard coming from the other elderly gamblers standing nearby. Mike could hear what she was saying and noticed that the whole group of them started in his direction. He began to get a little worried, as he didn't want to attract too much attention. He tensed up and began turning around looking for an escape route.

"Excuse me, young man," Janice said.

Mike looked at the security guard and then at the converging crowd. The security man smiled and just shrugged his shoulders as he said, "Well, I guess I'll leave you to your fan club while me and my partner take the bad guy upstairs and wait for the police to arrive."

"Hi, my name is Janice. And this is my best friend, Mary Slotki.

She saw you help stop the young man who attempted to steal my money."

Mike was taken aback by her and was feeling a little uncomfortable by her forwardness.

"I'm sorry, Janice, but I really don't think I had too much to do with it. I mean the security people were right on top of it, and—"

"Now, now, young man, don't be so modest. I know what I saw. If there were more people in the world like you then it would be a much safer place."

Mike was feeling really uncomfortable and all the attention was making it worse. It seemed to him that the whole casino was looking his way. He looked at the ladies and said, "I'm sorry, I really must be going." And with that he turned and started for the closest exit he could find.

The lady named Janis just stood there a little surprised by the way Mike responded to their compliment. "I swear I'll never understand that younger generation," she said and then grabbed her friend by the arm and led her in the direction of the crap tables.

Across the casino Melissa Conners and Adam Sheppard were nearing the exit when Melissa suddenly stopped in her tracks.

"What's the matter?" Adam asked.

"Oh, I was just wondering what all the commotion was about over there," she said as she craned her neck to get a better view in Mike's direction. "Let's take a look before we leave. Maybe somebody won something big and their luck will rub off."

Adam tried not to notice and was starting to get a little concerned that she was stalling.

"Okay, but let me call my driver to tell him we'll be a little—"

Adams words were cut short by the ringing of his cell.

"Hello," he said. His voice raised in a somewhat impatient manner, which startled Melissa into looking back at him.

"I know, I know, we'll be there in a moment." He looked at Melissa and realized his reply seemed out of character.

"It's my driver. He's waiting and the security people want him to leave. It seems they have a group coming and they need as much room as they can get at the door." He tried to look sheepishly apologetic as he said this hoping that he didn't spook Melissa.

"Oh, OK, I wouldn't want to get him into trouble," she said as she started once again in his direction. She turned around a few times as she walked, still trying to get a glimpse of what was going on. At one point, she saw the back of a man's head as he was trying to head for another exit. She suddenly had a feeling that there was something familiar about him or maybe his walk, but couldn't put her finger on it. She glanced forward at Adam and back again in the man's direction but he was gone. As they made their way through the exit, Lance Prescott stood in the background behind a row of slot machines and then followed them out the door to make sure they got into the waiting limo.

Mike Conners made a quick left after exiting the casino and started walking at a brisk pace. He couldn't shake the feeling that had started just after the security guards nabbed the thief and seemed to grow more intense as the two old ladies spoke with him. It was a cross between feeling like he was being watched and some kind of déjà vu. Knowing what he knew about his newfound abilities made him even more uneasy. He pictured people flying all over the place and crashing into walls and windows without him having any control over it. He shook the thought from his mind and continued his brisk pace.

When he came to the end of the block, he made another left and found himself in the front of the Excalibur. There were several limousines and busses picking up and dropping off customers. Mike didn't want to get in the middle of the crowd, so he decided to make his way across the street. He knew he would have to wait for an opening as it was just too crowded and dangerous. As he waited there he started looking at the tourists and couldn't help but wonder how much money each one of them was going to spend. He found himself studying individual faces and wondered what they were thinking.

Adam Sheppard reached for and opened the door to the car to let Melissa in. She thought it a little strange that the driver didn't open the door for them, but then thought it wasn't a regular limo with tinted windows and such but rather a large sedan. As she sat down, she noticed that there were two people in the front and neither one of them seemed to be dressed like a chauffeur should be. Before she could react or ask Adam who the other person was, she found him sliding in next to her and seemingly pushing her over.

He closed the door, looked at Melissa and said, "Excuse me, I didn't mean to bump you like that, I just thought you were in all the way." Melissa looking a little surprised and blushed slightly.

"It's OK, no big deal."

The driver made a slow U-turn and started off toward what Melissa hoped was a good meal and not a bad choice. As the car made its way through the maze of other vehicles to get to the main part of the strip, Melissa found herself looking at the people and wondering where they were all from. As they approached the intersection with Tropicana Avenue, she suddenly noticed a man wearing a red shirt walking at a fast pace in the same direction. There were many people walking along with him but not as fast and she noticed that he was weaving in and out of their way like some kind of running back on a football team attempting to make his way to the goal line. She wondered what the hurry was and attempted to view his face as her car passed him, but the other people walking blocked her sight. A few moments later the car suddenly came to a halt as traffic for this time of day often did. She was hoping that the man would catch up before they moved on.

"What are you looking at?" Adam asked.

Melissa turned to him and said, "Oh, I was just wondering about where all these people where from, and I couldn't help but notice one of them seemed to be rudely making his way through the rest of the crowd."

Adam moved closer to Melissa and tried to see if he could find the man she was referring to. As he did, he said, "Which one are you talking about?"

Melissa felt his closeness, which made her feel a little uneasy. She tried to ignore her uneasiness as she didn't want to seem helpless or afraid. Scanning the many people she finally saw the man still walking at the same speed. She still couldn't see his face but turned to Adam and said, "Look, it's that man with the red sh—" She was unable to finish the sentence. Just as she said this the crowd of people in front of him suddenly opened up and Melissa could see his face for the first time. Adam recognized him instantly and threw a look at Melissa to see her reaction. He could see her lips mouth the name Mike and knew she realized who he was. He could see her face and demeanor changing and knew he had to act quickly to prevent her from wanting to leave.

With the parting of the crowd, Mike couldn't help but see the car Melissa was in, right in front of him. The window of the car was coming down and she was staring back at him. For a moment it seemed as if all time had stopped and a fog of unconscionable proportions dulled his reactions. At the same moment Mike could see her and the realization of who she was suddenly stopped him in his tracks. A flood of memories and feelings he had not had for quite some time hammered at his subconscious and broke free. The rebirth of his memory and all that it held was a total shock to his system. He staggered to gain control of his balance as he continued to look at this woman who he now knew to be his wife. He suddenly saw a hand holding some kind of cloth come up to her face and pull her back away from the window as it closed. And with that, the car suddenly sped off.

What the hell, Mike thought as he continued to take control of himself. He looked around, a panicked look on his face. He tried to see what direction the car had gone but there were too many similar vehicles on the road. He moved over to a small flowered wall near the front of the building and sat on its edge trying to gain his composure. Mixed emotions of both joy and terror filled his body. His memory of his life, his marriage, the witness protection program, all had returned. It was as if a light bulb was suddenly turned on. He knew he needed to talk to someone. He needed to find out what was going on. He needed someone's help.

But who? he thought. *And what happened to the FBI?*

It was then the decision to contact the man he felt he could trust the most came to him.

Dr. Trumbull. I need to talk to him.

Mike stood up, still uneasy on his feet, and began to walk back to the hotel. He would go to his room and call the doctor.

Chapter 17

Lance Prescott stood by the elevator with one of his associates. He was looking down at his shiny patent leather shoes and talking on his cell phone to Adam.

"Yeah, I know. Don't hurt her anymore than you have to. I've got an idea on how to get them both together."

As he spoke, he looked up to see Mike walking in from outside.

"Alright, look, I got to go. He's here. Stay put at the warehouse."

Lance waited until Mike was right in front of the elevator door and had pressed the button to go up before moving to a position behind him. The doors opened up and Mike stepped inside with Lance right behind him. The associate waited outside to stop anyone else from using it. Mike turned around and saw the man stopping someone from getting on. He was about to say something when he heard Lance.

"Mike Conners?"

Lance's voice momentarily startled Mike, who turned and was now face to face with the man he recognized as the same one who gave his waiter a hard time and was watching him at the gambling tables earlier. For an instant he thought of trying to leave. Lance raised a leather case containing an official-looking badge and ID and said, "I'm Agent John Fleming of the Las Vegas office of the FBI."

The door to the elevator closed and Mike found himself alone with him as the car started going up. The two men looked at each other and at first Mike didn't know what to say. He had a lot of questions. At the moment the most important one was how the FBI knew where to find him. Lance, sensing Mike's concern, started right in to gain his trust and cooperation.

"I know you're probably wondering why I'm here or how I found you, but that's not important at the moment. You see, we have reason to believe that your wife Melissa has been abducted by some really bad people who want to get at you for reasons I'm sure you're aware of. We need to take you to a safe place until we can arrange her rescue and unite the two of you and get you both to a safe location within the witness protection program again."

Mike's mind was now racing, trying to fill in the gaps and trying to size up the agent. Lance could still see the puzzled look on Mike's face and so continued to talk.

"Look, my office received information that you and your wife had suddenly left the program and could be somewhere in Vegas. My orders are to secure your safe return to your handler and the program."

Mike saw his first opportunity to question Lance.

"OK, why isn't the agent who was assigned to me and my wife here then?"

"I'm sure you're aware of the necessity to keep the identities of agents, or handlers as we call them, as secret as possible. I'm not allowed to even know who he is. It's part of what makes the program so successful." Lance decided to change gears in an attempt to throw Mike off.

"Why did you and your wife skip out on the program?"

Mike looked at Lance trying to get a read on his sincerity, but was cut off when Lance continued. "The FBI takes great pride in providing this program, and if there was something you didn't like about it, then the two of you should have brought it to someone's attention."

Lance tried to sound as caring as possible. And he could see that Mike was softening.

"I don't know, I mean I can't really say. I...I haven't been myself. I was at the hospital till recently and I need to speak to one of the doctors there."

"Which doctor?" Lance asked.

"A Dr. Trumbull. At Las Vegas General. I had a problem with my memory and he was helping me."

"Okay, well look, I'll take you to a safe location and make arrangements for the doctor to come there. But you know we also have good doctors who could help you."

Mike leaned against the wall of the elevator to steady himself before answering, "I don't doubt that, it's just that I feel I'd really like to talk to Dr. Trumbull first."

"Alright, I'll make the arrangements as soon as we get you settled in."

The doors to the elevator opened on the fourth floor momentarily and then quickly closed as Lance pressed the button to go down.

Chapter 18

Jennifer Escalone surveyed the many monitors in the security office and was about to get up to get a drink of water, when she saw him. He was still in the elevator with another man and she quickly picked up a nearby phone and called the number on Agent Grant's business card.

"Hello."

"Agent Grant?"

"Yes, who is this?"

"It's Jennifer Escalone. I'm in the security office and I've spotted Mr. Conners. He's in the south tower elevator going down to the main floor. Do you want me to have my staff intercept him?"

Agent Grant was already in motion, waving for Bob Durham to follow, even before she had finished her question.

"No, just stay on the line with me and keep me abreast of his location as best you can. We're on our way."

"Alright."

The agents made their way to the elevator, which luckily was empty. Pressing the down button the two stood looking at each other. Bob Durham could sense the relief that Phil had as he continued his conversation with Ms. Escalone. The relief was short-lived however as the security officer kept talking.

"There is another man in the elevator with Mr. Conners and by his gestures it seems he knows him," Jennifer said. "They've reached the main floor and are heading towards the main entrance."

"What are they wearing?" Phil asked.

Phil Grant's elevator had another five floors to go and so he asked for some guidance as to the direction they should go when the doors opened and repeated as much information to Bob as he got.

"Mr. Conners has on a green shirt and blue jeans. The man he is with is dressed in a grey suit with a red tie. He has slicked backed black hair and he is shorter than Mr. Conners. Your elevator is actually closer to the entrance than theirs and so you might get to it before them. When you leave the elevator the doors will be to your right. Stand by, I have to look at another monitor to get a better view," Jennifer added.

Seconds later Agent Grant's elevator opened just as Jennifer continued, "OK they're on their way out the building and I've got only one more camera on the street in which to see them."

Phil and Bob pushed their way through the crowded lobby and out into the street all the time looking for them. They decided to split up and go in opposite directions and keep in contact with the small radios they each had.

The two agents could be seen jumping up and down in an effort to get a better view of the crowded streets in front of them.

At one point Bob thought he saw them and pulled out a small radio from his pocket to signal Phil. He was about to transmit when suddenly his own radio came alive with the sound of Phil's voice.

"Bob, I see them, they just got into a black Lincoln Town Car. I can't see the plate, but I'm going to follow."

As he said this, he realized that he needed a car. A limousine was just dropping off a couple at the curb with its driver standing outside when Phil intervened.

"Excuse me," he said to the driver, "but I need your vehicle."

As he said this he flashed his credentials with one hand and placed a business card into the chauffeur's breast pocket as he pushed him out of the way with his other hand and entered the vehicle. The chauffeur fell backwards slightly and onto the pavement. Before he could get up or say anything, Phil had closed the door and was pulling away from the curb. He tried to concentrate on the exact location of the Town Car he was following. The sound of Bob's voice suddenly broke his concentration.

"Phil, where are you, buddy?"

"Sorry I couldn't wait for you, Bob. I'm following the limo and we're headed west on Tropicana Avenue. I'll keep you posted."

"That's just great, I'm getting our car and I'll follow so don't get all Rambo on me and go it alone."

"Yeah, 10-4," was the last thing Bob heard before heading for the parking garage for their vehicle.

Traffic was fairly heavy and Phil knew he would have to drive aggressively to keep from losing sight of the Town Car. He also knew not to be spotted. He wished Bob was closer with their other vehicle so they could switch off with each other to avoid detection.

The Town Car made a left onto South Rainbow Boulevard and Phil tried to radio Bob with the new directions, but all he heard was static. He figured Bob must still be in the garage area and the walls were stopping his transmission. Traffic began to get lighter and speed up slightly. Phil found himself trying to remember the names of the various roads they passed but couldn't read all of them.

Traffic grew even lighter as they moved away from the main part of the city. Phil was able to make out the plate number and noticed a local radio station bumper sticker for KOMP 92.3. The red and gold lettering was easier to spot than the numbers on the license plate. The Town Car began to accelerate more and was doing about seventy miles an hour. Phil decided to let more space get between them as traffic became lighter and he became more noticeable. Phil was about a quarter of a mile behind when suddenly he saw the Town Car slow down rapidly and pull off to the side of the road. This was just the maneuver Phil was worried about. He would be on them in seconds. He knew that his best course of action would be to just go right past them and see what developed. Any sudden stop by him would surely tip off the driver of the Town Car that he was being followed. He was relieved that the limo had tinted windows. He slowed down slightly but not enough to be noticeable. As Phil moved passed the Town Car he made a conscious effort to not look directly at them. Phil could see an intersection was coming up. He decided to make a left turn there at West Sunset Road.

As soon as Agent Grant made the turn, he noticed an old building on the right side of the road about two hundred feet from the intersection. Turning the wheel sharply to his right, he maneuvered the limo behind the building and out of sight from the roadway. Phil left the car running as he exited and ran to a point where he had a good view of the intersection. The moments dragged on and Phil began to worry that the Town Car had turned around. He was just about to go back to the car and retrace his steps when he saw the Town Car make a right at the intersection and head west on Sunset Road. He knew it had to be the same car as he noticed the same red and gold bumper sticker for a local radio station. Jumping back into the limo, Phil was soon following again. Phil decided it might be a good time to contact Agent Durham on the radio.

He reached into his pocket, but couldn't locate it.

He looked around on the seat next to him and anywhere else within his reach that it might be, but was unable to locate it.

Shit. Just what I need, he thought. He was about to try his cell phone but then decided to wait until he knew where they were going. Phil didn't have long to wait, for the Town Car slowed and turned right onto a dirt road that led to what appeared to be a small warehouse on the corner where Sunset intersects with Durango Drive.

Chapter 19

Mike Conners suddenly sat up as he noticed they were stopping.

"What is this place?" he asked.

Lance did not look at him but instead kept staring out the window.

"Agent Fleming," Mike said with a louder voice.

Turning slowly to face Mike, Lance answered. "This is the place I mentioned to you. You'll be safe here until we can get you and your wife back in the program."

"I thought we were going to a regular house, like what my wife and I were used to."

"That will come in the near future. For now, and until we get your wife back, this is more secure."

"Speaking of Melissa, you never told me about who might have taken her or how they got to her. The last I remember, she was safe in a house the FBI sent us to."

Lance could sense that Mike was trying to test his knowledge of what Mike new to be the truth and so he chose his words carefully.

"Look, Mr. Conners, I already told you that a lot of what the

FBI does to protect the security of those it protects is known on a need-to-know basis. I myself don't have a lot of answers for you at this time as my assignment was just to find you and bring you to a safe location."

Looking around, Mike was not sure of what to believe. This place didn't seem like the kind of a place the FBI would use for such things. He only knew he needed help to get reunited with his wife and for now this Agent Fleming seemed his only solution.

The man in the front passenger seat got out and opened the door for Mike. As he exited the Town Car, Lance came around from his side.

"Okay, Mr. Conners, let's get inside."

Closing the car door, the man led the way followed by Lance walking alongside Mike.

As they got closer, Mike could see a man looking out at them from a small window in the door. When the door opened Mike could feel the cool air of the air-conditioned building flow out to great them. The brightness of the day made it impossible to see inside. And as Mike entered he had to stop to have his eyes adjust to the light. He took maybe three steps further before he felt the sharp pain of the slap jack as it made contact with the back of his head. He tried to turn to see what had happened but a second blow to the head made him crash to the ground.

Chapter 20

Agent Grant drove past the road and made a left onto Durango and then stopped just before where it intersected with State Route 215. He figured it was about a quarter of a mile from where he was to the warehouse. He would have to leave the car and walk so as not to be detected.

He placed his cell phone in his pocket as he exited the limo and began to make his way back towards the warehouse.

The sun was high overhead and the heat of the day made Phil wish he wasn't wearing a suit jacket. He didn't want to take it off as it would expose his service weapon and holster. He walked about fifty yards before crossing the street to get a better view of the area around the warehouse. There was no movement of any kind that he could see. The property was not fenced and the side that he would be approaching from had several windows high up and almost to the roof. There was a row of smaller storage containers and a dumpster that Phil thought would help him get closer without being detected. Taking his cell phone out of his pocket, he entered Agent Durham's number and waited for a response.

"Hello."

"Yeah, Bob, it's me."

"It's about time you called; I've been trying to reach you on the radio."

"I must have lost it somewhere along the way. Where are now?"

"I'm still on Tropicana Avenue. I didn't want to travel too far as I had no idea where you went from the casino."

"Alright. I followed the car Mike was in to a warehouse on the corner of West Sunset and South Durango Drive. Its west of the strip. I'll wait here for you so try to hurry," Phil said.

Phil waited for a reply but all he heard was the beeping of his cell which told him they were disconnected.

Dammed cell phones, they never work when you need them, he thought. Placing his cell back in his pocket, he began to maneuver closer to the building.

He crossed Sunset and then noticed a drainage ditch about three feet deep, which if taken, would bring him to about forty feet from the rear of the warehouse. The ditch was dry due to lack of rain. From there it was about another twenty feet to the first of the two storage buildings he viewed earlier. Phil jumped down into the ditch and began to trot towards the building, keeping as low a profile as he could. The dust from the ditch was kicking up around him and so he decided to slow up. It was a good idea, for just as he did, he looked down and noticed there in front of him was a rather large rattlesnake blocking his path. The ditch was very narrow at this spot, which left little room for Phil to move around the snake. He didn't want to climb out of the ditch for fear of someone seeing him. His only option was to chase the serpent away. Bending over, he picked up a small stone and tossed it. The stone landed in front of the snake which caused it to just retract into a tight coil that most snakes use as a fighting position. Phil decided to try again, this time hitting the snake square in the face.

It spit and lunged at the rock but did not actually bite it. The snake began to move sideways up the side of the ditch, but could only go so far before it would slip back down again. Phil started to kick dirt at it but then stopped for fear of making too much dust which might attract attention. At one point the snake actually started to move towards Phil and he found himself backing up. The thought occurred to him that he might have to discard his jacket and toss it over the snake. He would take off his shoulder holster and stick his service weapon in his waist. He was about to do that when the snake started to slither away from him. Phil followed slowly behind and then noticed the snake disappear into a pipe that appeared to be a drainage pipe for the building. He was thankful that obstacle was out of the way.

Phil continued making his way closer to the building. When he got to an area he felt was closest to one of the storage buildings, he stopped to get a better view of where he wanted to go. He carefully peered out from the ditch and figured he had about fifteen feet of open space before the building would hide him. He scrambled up out of the ditch and sprinted to the first storage building. It was a small structure made of metal with no windows and one door. Phil could feel the heat coming off of the building and wondered what might be inside. Peering from behind it, he could see a trash dumpster and a second storage building, slightly bigger than the first and more to his right. The parking area was to the right of that and Phil could see the Town Car parked there. There was no one in the car that he could see. A black cargo van was parked next to it. This building blocked his view of the door to warehouse itself, and offered what he felt was a good spot in which to get inside. Again Phil sprinted to this other building and then stopped to plan his next move. He took his cell phone out and was going to call Agent Durham to give him an update. There were no bars on the screen, and thus no service.

Shit, that figures, he thought. *Now what do I do?*

Looking around and seeing no security cameras or anyone guarding the entrance, he made his decision. He felt it would be best to approach from an angle to prevent anyone inside from seeing him through the window in the door.

He hesitated for a moment before whispering to himself, "I must be crazy, but what the hell." With that he moved towards the door to the warehouse.

He bent down and tried to listen for any noise that came from within. Not hearing anything, he tried the door and was surprised to see it was not locked. Opening it, he slipped inside. It was fairly dark, and so Phil kept low and moved to an area to his right. A row of crates was stacked in front of him and he made his way to a position between them and the wall. He decided to stay there to get his eyes used to the light and try and gather any other information about this place he could. He sat there and could hear the faint sounds of people talking, but could not figure out which direction it was coming from. As soon as he could see better, he moved to the end of the line of crates and peered around them to view the surroundings. There was a row of glass-lined office cubicles on the far wall which was only about one hundred feet from him. Two of the offices had light coming from the windows, and he could make out people milling around inside. There was one man sitting on a chair next to a door with no windows to the left of one of the offices. In between, Phil could see other crates, stacked to the ceiling, lined up in neat rows with foreign writing on them. A catwalk near the ceiling lined three of the walls of the building, and Phil knew he would have to be careful. From where he was, no one appeared to be up there. He needed to hear what was being said and decided to use these crates to get closer to the offices. He backtracked to the other end of the crates as it would be easier to sneak closer from there without being detected.

Pulling his service weapon from its holster, he began maneuvering between the crates to get closer. He made it past the second row and stopped to listen. The talking he heard before had stopped and no other sound could be heard. From this new position he could still see the catwalk. After waiting for several minutes in the dead silence, he began to get a nervous feeling in the pit of his stomach. He decided he shouldn't wait any longer and inched toward the end of the crates to get a better look. Peering around the corner, he could see the same offices, but this time the lights were out and the doors were closed.

Where'd everyone go? he thought. He was about to retrace his steps when all of a sudden the sound of his cell phone broke the silence. Panic and anger filled him for not turning it off before entering the building. He reached into his pocket to silence it and at the same time he turned to get out as fast as he could. He made it halfway down the row of crates before the building came alive with the sounds of men running and a voice yelling orders to secure the building. All the lights in the place came on at once, and Phil checked his weapon to be sure the safety was off. He heard a noise behind him and turned to see a man pointing a shotgun at him from maybe twenty feet away. He brought his weapon up to fire as the man ducked behind the crates. In the same instance, the voice of Lance Prescott and the sickening sound of a shotgun as it racked a round into a chamber could be heard coming from the other end of the row of crates.

"Okay, asshole, don't move or you're dead."

Chapter 21

Melissa Conners awoke from her drug-induced nap on the floor of the warehouse. She sat up and tried to focus her eyes on her surroundings. The room Adam Sheppard placed her in was small and smelled musty. She could see a row of dirty windows high up near the ceiling. They did not let much light in. The door to the room was directly in front of her. She felt like she had been out all night partying on cheap booze. Nauseating feelings of impending doom brought her to the brink of tears. As she sat there, she became more aware of what happened. She inspected herself, first looking at her clothes and then checking to make sure she was not violated sexually. Only after she was satisfied of this, did she allow herself to cry. It started as a small whimper and soon rose to uncontrollable sobbing. She would only allow herself a few moments of this before she again regained her composure. The crying seemed to act as a cleansing agent. For as soon as she stopped, her head cleared and she was able to look around and see the rest of the room. There was a small chair near the wall to her right and over in the opposite corner she saw what looked like an old mattress with a mound of blankets on it. She rose to her feet, her left hand moving to the wall to keep her balance. Once she felt steady enough, she walked towards the mattress. As she got closer, she thought she heard a low audible groaning sound and realized the blanket moved slightly. The sudden fear of not knowing what caused this stopped her in her tracks. She tried desperately to focus on the mattress, but knew she would have to go closer to see. She inched towards it and only when she was within eight feet of it was she able to make out the form of a person. She stood there frozen with fear, not knowing what to do. She was about to retreat to the area where the chair was when the person rolled and groaned slightly again. She could see it was a man but the shadows of the room did not allow for her to see him clearly. Judging by his sounds she could only imagine he was hurt or injured in some way. She decided that maybe she should go closer still to get a better look. Cautiously she made her way to an angle that gave her a better view of his face. As she did, something familiar about his features took shape in her mind. Before she realized it, she was almost on top of him. Looking down, she suddenly felt weak in the knees. Her breathing increased and the anxiety of the moment caused her to find herself slumping down to a position next to him.

"Oh, my God, Mike," she softly whispered.

She sat there looking at him, wondering if maybe this was all some weird dream caused by the drug she was subjected to. She shook her head in disbelief, and only then did she realize that tears were streaming down her face. Melissa leaned over and held him briefly before straightening. She took his hand and softly whispered to him again,

"Mike, what happened; where have you been?"

Chapter 22

As far back as he could remember dreams were things that Mike did not have. He couldn't remember the last time he had one. Yet as far as he was concerned, this appeared to be one. That was the only explanation his injured psyche could muster.

Mike looked at this person looking back at him. His judgment was fogged by the injuries. His mind desperately wanted an answer to what he saw. Was he imagining this? Was it a cruel joke? He blinked and found himself reaching out to touch the arm of what he hoped was not an illusion. At the same time he heard her call his name. It was only then that the reality of this experience took hold and for the first time in a long time Mike felt what he had missed all too much.

"Melissa?" he gently whispered.

He rose up onto his elbows, and a sharp pain shooting through the back of his neck made him groan slightly.

"Melissa, my God, it's really you!"

With that the two of them came together in a warm embrace that made them both forget their pain.

Pulling away and looking in Mike's eyes, Melissa could feel her emotions once again tipping the scales between anger and hurt. She had many questions that needed to be answered.

"I can't believe this. Mike, I've missed you so much. Why did you leave, and where did you go? How could you not have tried to contact me?" she rambled.

Mike raised his outstretched hand and gently touched her lips with his fingertips.

"Shhh!" he whispered. "I wish I could tell you. I wish I could give you all the answers to all your questions, but I can't. And the reason why is that I don't know."

"What do you mean, how could you not know?" she asked as she shifted her position slightly.

Mike wrinkled his brow and looked down, closing his eyes slightly and then looked back up as he took her hands in his.

"Honey, the last thing I remember was driving to work early one morning. There was no one else on the road. I was listening to the radio when all of a sudden, the station I was listening to was drowned out by this high-pitched whining noise. I changed the station, but all I could get was the same noise. I shut the radio off, and it was only then that I realized it wasn't the radio at all because I could still hear it. The noise was coming from outside the car. I pulled off the road and then the noise became ear-splitting. I placed my hands over my ears and as I did, I could see the whole interior of the car suddenly filled with the brightest light you could imagine. That was the last moment I could recall. The next thing I knew I was walking around in the desert outside Las Vegas. A truck driver found me and brought me to a hospital."

Mike stopped there and looked into Melissa's eyes to determine her response. She sat there blinking, her mouth wide open like some baby bird waiting to be fed by its mother.

Mike squeezed her hand slightly. "Melissa...honey"

She closed her mouth and looked back at him.

"I...I don't know what to say. It sounds so incredible. Do you have any idea how long you were gone?" She did not let him answer before blurting out, "Over four months."

"I have no memory of that time," he said. "None"

The two of them just kept looking at each other for what seemed an eternity, before Mike felt compelled to continue. He explained about his time in the hospital as best he could and how bits and pieces of his memory would return. He didn't want to burden her with too much information about things he couldn't himself explain and so he left out the parts about some of his strange talents. After they brought each other up to date on their time spent apart, the conversation turned to their more pressing situation.

"So, how did you get here?" Mike asked.

"I guess you could say I was too trusting and stupid. I mean this guy, this Adam Sheppard." She stopped herself when she realized that what she was about to say sounded like she was going to be unfaithful to him, but then knowing that wasn't the case continued. "He was going to show me around Vegas. That's all."

Mike saw the hurt in her eyes and the sound of her voice gave him a sense of relief. He knew she loved him and even being apart for so long, she wasn't the type to be unfaithful. Grabbing her by the shoulders and looking into her eyes he said, "Melissa, honey, don't get down on yourself. You weren't the only one duped into reacting the way you did. I thought the guy who brought me here was from the FBI. He gave me some story about how they felt you were captured by the very people the FBI was supposed to be protecting us from. Turns out that he was the bad people."

With a slight sigh, Melissa grabbed Mike once again and held him in her arms. The two of them sat there in silence rocking slowly back and forth. Mike then cradled her face in his hands and kissed her slowly and lightly at first and then deeply and more meaningful. His pain had disappeared and a new sense of oneness with Melissa took over. They were two minutes into their passion when footsteps and voices could be heard coming from outside the room. Pulling apart, they turned to face the door as it opened. A light from above suddenly illuminated the room and through the doorway stumbled Agent Phil Grant as he was pushed by Lance Prescott and Adam Sheppard. A third man also entered cradling a mac ten firearm.

Melissa and Mike both jumped to there feet.

Chapter 23

It took Mike a few seconds to realize who he was before responding.

"Agent Grant?"

"You recognize me?"

"Yes I do. What's going on?"

"Shut up, stupid, and sit down," Lance snapped. He threw a quick look at Melissa. "You too, gorgeous."

Turning back to Mike, he continued. "I guess by now you figured out, I'm not FBI."

"Yeah, the pain on the back of my head kind of convinced me of that. So who are you guys?"

Phil Grant answered for him. "They're the people I was supposed to protect you and Melissa from," he said as he walked over to where they were standing.

"I don't recognize any of them," Mike said.

Phil looking straight at Lance said, "This is Lance Prescott. He and this other guy work for Drew Swindell."

"I prefer to call Drew my associate," Lance added.

Mike and Melissa looked at each other and then at Phil who added, "My guess is he recognized the two of you as you showed up at the Excalibur."

"Yeah, I remembered Mike from the trial, and an office party. I lost a lot of money because of you," he said as he pointed his stubby fingers at Mike.

"I couldn't believe my eyes when I saw Mike at a crap table with the luckiest streak I've seen in a while. As soon as I recognized him, I just had to contact Drew with the good news. Then when your lovely wife showed up there also, I thought wow, talk about luck."

Melissa looking confused asked, "I've never seen you or met you. How did you know who I was?"

"I guess you don't remember me from some of the company parties back in New York that you and Mike attended, before the problems Mike caused with the investment firm."

Mike looked at Drew with renewed interest. He decided that there was indeed something familiar about him but back then he had met so many people in the course of his work that he just couldn't be sure.

"I didn't cause and wasn't the cause of those troubles you're talking about," Mike said. "You guys caused your own problems. I was just the one caught in the middle of it."

"Yeah, well, you should have kept your mouth shut and remained loyal to Mr. Swindell."

Phil turned to Mike and tried to reassure him of his actions.

"You did the right thing back then, Mike. Don't let him get to you."

Drew looked at Agent Grant with a look of disgust and said, "You can say what you want; in a little while it won't matter anyway. As soon as I get the word from Mr. Swindell, you guys are history."

Melissa inhaled a short breath while grabbing Mike's arm and blurted out, "What."

Mike could see the look of fear in her eyes, and while trying not to show his own, he held her close to comfort her.

Phil looked at Drew and knew what he meant. He thought their only hope was that his partner would somehow get there first.

Lance pointed at Agent Grant and said, "You can stay here with your two buddies till I get the word and then we'll be back." With that, the three backed out of the room and locking the door behind them.

Phil and Mike looked at each other. Neither of them had to say what they felt. Melissa began to shake with fear and Mike held her tight.

"It's going to be alright, honey," he said as he looked at Phil for some sort of agreement.

Phil had to look away in disgust. He was mad at himself for failing to keep Mike and Melissa safe.

"I was in contact with my partner just before I arrived. I gave him the heads-up as to where this place is. It should only be a matter of minutes before he arrives with help," Phil said as he tried to sound as convincing as possible.

"I hope you're right," Mike added.

Agent Grant began walking around the room inspecting it to see if there was any way to reach the windows at the top of the room.

After deciding that there wasn't, he began to formulate a plan of attack as best he could for when they returned.

He walked over to the mattress and lifted it up, propping it next to the door.

"What are you doing?" Mike asked.

"I don't know how much time we have. And just in case my partner is delayed, I want to give us every opportunity that we can to get out of here in one piece."

Agent Grant then walked over to the chair and moved it to the corner behind the door, which opened inward, so that it was hidden from direct view when someone entered.

"Melissa, I want you to crouch down behind this chair keeping it in front of you as best you can. Mike, I want you to stand behind me. When they open the door, we'll use the mattress as a shield while we crash into them. I'm hoping that it will give me enough time to get to the guy with the gun."

Mike thought about Phil's plan while he looked at Melissa standing in the corner trembling in fear. He found himself doubting a successful outcome and then the realization of losing all he had and all he loved made him start to breathe heavily. Phil, sensing his emotion, tried to calm him. He knew his plan might work but he needed Mike to control himself. He walked over to him, placed a hand on shoulder and said, "Look, I know this is hard, but I need you to do this. Melissa needs you to do this."

Mike lowered his head as he shook it back and forth, took a deep breath and let it out slowly. "OK," he said.

"There's one more thing I want to do to give us an advantage."

Taking one shoe off, Phil stepped back and launched it at the overhead light fixture like a pro football quarterback going for the win. It found its mark as the fluorescent bulbs burst and rained down on the floor below. The room was instantly turned back to the way it was before Phil arrived. All that remained to do now was wait. Phil stayed by the door as Mike made his way to Melissa to comfort her again.

Five minutes passed, but seemed like five years. In that time Mike began to think back to the events of the passed few days. He thought of Agent Grant and how he interviewed him at the hospital under the guise of a doctor and wondered why he didn't tell him who he really was. He thought if he had then maybe his memory would have returned sooner and he might not be in this spot. He thought of the people he met and the events that took place that he had no explanation for. But mostly he thought of

Melissa and how much he loved her and that he hoped their lives could somehow become normal again.

Footsteps could be heard and Phil motioned for Mike to get behind him. He could hear Mike's kiss and the words "I love you" being said in unison as the two separated for what Phil hoped weren't their last. Waiting for the door to open, Phil and Mike crouched down low, like two leopards waiting for their prey.

Chapter 24

The sounds of the key entering and turning the lock seemed louder than could be possible, and in that moment the slightest bit of doubt somehow crept into Mike's head.

The door suddenly opened and one of Drew Swindle's men entered, carrying a mach ten semi auto. He took two short steps forward and was about to push the door all the way open when Phil sprang into action. He slammed into the man, pinning him between the mattress and the steel door. The force of his charge caused the weapon to fire off a burst of bullets in a loud crescendo which ricocheted around the room. The gun dislodged and fell to the floor to Agent Grant's right. Phil scrambled for it and just as he did, a second loud shot rang out from somewhere behind him. The bullet tore through him and caused him to wince in pain. He grabbed his shoulder, preventing him from taking complete control of the weapon.

Before he could recover, two other men were on him. One wrestled the gun away while the second pummeled Phil with his fists. Mike retreating to the area where Melissa was, grabbed her and held her tightly in his arms. "I'm sorry, honey," he whispered as if to blame himself for not helping more. Phil looked up at the two men and then at Mike before lowering himself into a kneeling position.

"Aw, shit, it hurts," he said.

Lance Prescott slowly walked in and said, "That ain't nothing compared to the pain that's coming."

The man who Phil surprised got up slowly and walked over to where Phil knelt and kicked him in the side. The sickening sound of ribs breaking could be heard as Phil groaned in pain. Melissa could be heard crying and her whimpering seemed to arouse something inside of Lance. He looked at her with a crazed look in his eyes. Pointing to Agent Grant, Lance said, "Take him out and put him in one of the chairs. Then come back for cutie and tattle-tale boy."

Mike held her tighter and the look of fear on her face made him feel sick inside. He started to realize that this might be the last time he held her. The fear of what might happen next caused him to start to shake. As he tried to control his body, he suddenly became aware of a low-pitched humming sound.

The men came back into the room and took both Mike and Melissa by the arm and pulled them away from each other.

"Please don't hurt us," Melissa pleaded.

They were brought out to an area that had three chairs set against the wall. Agent Grant was already secured to one of them. Mike could see him lowering his head and grimacing with pain from what had just taken place. Mike was placed in one and had his arms and legs secured to it with duct tape.

Phil looked at Mike and Melissa and knew their future as well as his was indeed finished unless Agent Durham would show up. He looked at Lance and decided that maybe he could reason with him to buy some time.

"You know you're not going to get away with whatever you have planned. If you let us go now I'll do what I can to make it easier on you."

Lance looked at Phil with raised eyebrows. His mouth dropped open and he laughed out loud in a most sinister way. He looked at Adam Sheppard and said, "Do you believe this guy?"

He then walked over to where Phil was, slowly bent down and whispered in his ear, "Planned? I don't have anything planned. I'm just going by what feels good at the moment. It's a shame you guys didn't do a better job of protecting these people. I think as we go along you'll enjoy the fact that I've decided to kill you last just so you can really feel like a failure."

Agent Grant, at the risk of being unprofessional, stared him straight in his face and whispered back, "Fuck you, asshole!"

Lance straightened up just as slowly and laughed out loud in a mocking manner.

Adam Sheppard was standing next to Melissa staring at her with a look that made her cringe inside. He turned to Lance and said, "What do you think, boss?" as he grabbed her by the back of her hair and pulled her head back.

"Do you want to do her or should I?"

Melissa let out a short whimper, half from the pain and half from fear.

"What—no—don't hurt her!" Mike screamed.

"Wow, look who's suddenly getting balls," Lance added as he walked over to stand next to Adam and Melissa.

"If you're going to do anything, do it to me instead. I'm the one who caused you problems, not her."

"It doesn't work that way," Lance smirked. "Even if I wanted to, all three of you have seen too much. No, I'm afraid we're just gonna do what we're gonna do."

Mike struggled with the tape even though he knew it was hopeless. Adam, still holding onto Melissa's hair, led her over to a set of pipes that were about a foot over her head. He motioned for one of the other men to help him as he tied her arms above her and to the pipes.

"Please, no!" she said as she tried to resist as best she could without success.

Mike sat there watching this and couldn't believe what was happening.

Lance and Adam looked at each other and both laughed low and in a weird way that made Phil cringe with the thought of what they might be planning.

"You guys are sick," Phil said in a low voice as he struggled against the pain he was feeling.

"What did you say?" Lance replied, as he shot a look at him.

"Okay, Adam. Let's show our guest what sick really is."

"Sure, my pleasure," he said.

Adam walked very slowly around Melissa staring at her, a deep sinister stare right into her eyes that she could feel in the depths of her soul. She tried to follow his movements as best she could. On his second time around, he came to a complete stop behind her and moved in with his body leaning against her. She whimpered in fear, which seemed to arouse him even more. He then reached up and started to caress her breasts through her clothes.

"No, please don't," she pleaded.

"Oh, I'm sorry, maybe this will feel better," he said and then he ripped her blouse open, exposing her bra.

"You bastards," Mike yelled.

Adam then walked around to the front of her and Mike could see that he now had a knife in his hand. He placed it up in between her breasts and sliced away the middle of her bra, exposing her.

Adam then cut away the rest of it and her blouse so that she was bare from the waist up.

Melissa was crying uncontrollably as she looked at Mike, and then at Agent Grant, who had lost a lot of blood and had all he could do to just stay conscious.

Mike watched as Adam then began sucking on Melissa's breasts and began undoing her pants.

"Fucking bastards!" Mike yelled.

Lance stood there watching and smiling. The other men laughed and one could be heard chanting, "Go, Adam, go," like some kind of fan at a football game seeing the running back going for a touchdown.

Mike was struggling and crying with fear. As he watched the events unfolding before him, he couldn't make sense of it all.

Suddenly he became acutely aware of the low-pitched noise again which was now getting louder. He found himself shaking his head as if to clear it as he tried to focus his attention on his wife through teary, blurred eyes. The lights in the warehouse also started flickering and then getting brighter. Lance noticed it and sent one of his men to go check the circuit breakers. It was then that the events of the past few days made him realize and remember what this noise might be. The last time it happened at the hospital, it caused the furniture to move and FBI agent Tom Martin to get hurt. He thought maybe, just maybe, if he could control it, he might be able to put an end to this nightmare.

Mike looked down at his arms taped to the chair and began to concentrate on his bindings. He pictured them in his mind being undone and ripped away. The sound of Melissa screaming in fear made him look at her, breaking his concentration. The sight of her helplessly hanging there and the thought of her being defiled were too much for him to bear. As he watched Adam start to slowly pull down her pants, he found himself losing control and shaking. The room suddenly took on an eerie bluish-green tint and then it happened. The chair beneath Mike collapsed into many pieces as the tape on his arms and legs seemed to disintegrate and fall off. Mike slowly stood up, his eyes bulging with a maddened sense of hate for his captors. Lance looked around at the eerie color of the room and wondered what was going on. He noticed Mike standing there staring and couldn't believe what he saw.

"What the hell is happening?" Lance asked as he motioned for the other man to get Mike.

The man took one step in Mike's direction and that was as far as he got. Mike raised and opened his hand toward him, sending him flying through the air and striking the far wall about ten feet off the ground before falling to the floor in a heap of dead flesh. Lance, his mouth wide open, followed the flight of his associate and shook his head in disbelief. Turning his attention now to Adam, Mike opened his outstretched hands toward him, causing him to be lifted up in the air about eight feet. The sound of bones cracking could be heard as Mike then closed his hands into a tight fist as if to crush the life out of him. Adam screamed in pain and fell to the floor, blood flowing from his mouth and ears.

Lance looked at his fallen friend and then at Mike. He couldn't believe what he just witnessed. Half filled with rage and half with fear, he pulled a gun from his waist and raised it towards Mike. He suddenly felt his arm go stiff and was unable to point it in his direction. The gun and Lance's arm began to twist and turn as if some unknown invisible assailant had grabbed him. Lance stood there trying to control his arm without success. He tried to pull back as his fear took over and he wanted to run from the room. Suddenly, he realized that he couldn't run as he was no longer on the ground. Looking down, he could see that he was now suspended in the air some five feet. He looked at Mike who appeared to be basked in an eerie greenish-blue light smiling back at him. The gun he held was now pointing squarely at his own chest. Lance stared at his weapon in disbelief and Mike could see him mouth the words, "Oh, shit."

That was the last thing he was able to do before the sound of his gun firing echoed off the walls of the room And Lance fell to the floor, his body quivered slightly before his life left him.

Melissa screamed Mike's name and the sound of her voice brought him out of his trance. He picked up the knife that Adam had dropped at her feet and cut the tape that held her.

"Oh, Mike, I love you so much," she said as she collapsed into his arms. Mike gently placed her on the ground and then went to the other room, retrieved a blanket from the mattress and returned to bundle her trembling body. He held her in his arms caressing her hair.

"It's alright, sweetheart. No one's going to hurt you again."

Melissa moaned and looked around at Lance on the ground then asked, "What happened to him? How did you get free?"

Mike hesitated to answer at first but then asked, "Don't you know? I mean didn't you—"

Melissa cut him off. "I must have blacked out. The last thing I remember that disgusting creep was…"

She couldn't finish the sentence and broke down into tears as the reality of the experience took hold.

Mike held her closely as he rocked her back and forth to comfort her. It was then that he remembered Agent Grant who was slumped over unconscious in the chair. He left Melissa momentarily and cut him free. As he checked for a pulse, Phil stirred and tried to focus on him.

"Mike, is that you?"

"Agent Grant, don't move too much. You've lost a lot of blood. I'm going to go for help."

As he said this, Phil looked around and saw Lance on the ground.

He was about to ask what happened when all of a sudden they could hear many footsteps approaching from the other end of the warehouse. Mike backed away from Agent Grant and prepared himself by facing in that direction. He raised his hands in front of him but before he could react, he heard a man's voice yell out, "Phil, where are you?"

Agent Grant, recognizing the sound of his partner, Robert Durham, answered weakly, "We're back here."

"Oh, thank God help has finally arrived," Mike said as he relaxed his stance and went to meet them as they entered the area.

"Agent Grant's been shot and needs an ambulance," he said.

Agent Durham and several other agents along with a contingent of police officers quickly entered and secured the area. Robert, after seeing that there was no longer a threat from Lance or his men, went right past Mike to where his partner sat. Looking at the dead man near him, he said, "I guess you've got everything under control here, buddy."

Phil looked up at him and tried to stand as he said, "Very funny. What took you—" before collapsing back down.

"Wow, brother, just take it easy. The ambulance will be here shortly. You got to get fixed up 'cause judging by this mess you'll have a ton of paperwork to complete."

Agent Durham, after looking around, asked, "How did you manage to get the drop on these guys?"

Phil looked up and tried to focus on the room. He looked at Mike holding his wife as a medical technician started working on him, getting him ready for transport to a hospital.

"I honestly don't know, Bob. The last thing I remember was sitting in this chair unable to move as Lance and his men were starting to have their way with Melissa. I blacked out and the next thing I know, Mike is kneeling next to me cutting the tape from my arms."

Bob slowly lifted his gaze into Mike's direction as Mike looked back.

"You mean Mike did this? I find that hard to believe. But, geez, he's the only one here." His voice trailed off as he started inspecting the room further.

Mike, sensing the agent was looking for answers, turned his attention once again to Melissa who also was then being looked at by a medical technician.

Agent Durham walked slowly over to where Mike and Melissa were and stood there while the medical team finished looking after them.

"How are they doing?" he asked.

The technician, who was kneeling next to Melissa, stood up to answer him. "Not bad. Mr. Conners has a nasty bump to the back of his head which I would think should be x-rayed and the missus has some tissue damage to her wrists. Aside from that and her stressful experience, she should be fine."

"Good to hear," Bob said as he smiled at Mike and Melissa trying to make them feel better about all that happened.

"Mr. Conners, my team and I will escort you and Melissa to the hospital for that. We'll have a secure area set up for you. After the debriefing we'll need to get the two of you back into the program at a different location."

Mike, with a perplexed look, asked, "Debriefing, what do you mean?"

"Well, I'm sure you can understand we have some questions as to what happened here at the warehouse. And we'd also like to help you remember what happened to you and where you were those months before you resurfaced."

Mike looked down momentarily at the floor and shook his head slightly before raising it back to ask, "Are we going to Las

Vegas, General? I mean, I would prefer it as there is a Dr. Trumbull there I can trust."

"I'm aware of the fact that Dr. Trumbull was treating you up to the time you left the hospital. We have our own specialist that might be better for you and—"

Mike cut him off abruptly. "No, I don't feel comfortable with that."

Agent Grant, who was listening, looked at his partner and said, "Bob, I think for the time being we should make an exception about who helps Mike out here. From what I know of Dr. Trumbull, he's quite qualified for the job."

"Alright. I'll make further arrangements," Bob said as the medical technicians started to transport Agent Grant, Mike and Melissa to the hospital.

Epilogue

Melissa Conners sat at the desk in her living room looking out at the beautiful view of the ocean. She had just finished writing a letter to her mother and father. She addressed the envelope and only after she placed a stamp on it did she realize the return address was wrong.

"Ah, shit, that's the second time I did that today," she said.

Mike looked up from the newspaper he was reading, smiled, and said, "Second time you did what?"

"Put the wrong return address on an envelope."

"No big deal. We've only been here five weeks."

"Yeah, but you would think that would be enough time to get the old address out of my head," she replied.

Mike got up from the chair and moved behind her. His hands began to massage her shoulders and neck as he offered her a suggestion.

"Wanna go for a walk?"

"Walk," she said in a whimsical way as she stood up, turned around, and placed her hands on his waist. "I can think of a much better way to relieve stress."

"Yeah, me too," he said as the two of them came together in

a passionate kiss. He pulled back but kept her hand as he started for the bedroom. They were halfway there when the sound of the doorbell stopped them in their tracks. They looked at each other, each seemingly knowing what they were going to say beforehand.

"I know, I know," Mike said as he let go of her and walked slowly toward the front door. He looked through the peephole, a habit he picked up since their run-in with people from their previous life. The man behind the door was facing away from him, but Mike knew who it was anyway. He turned briefly to Melissa and said, "Dr. Trumbull. His timing sucks."

Melissa pouted and then smiled slightly. She knew they were both disappointed in his timing but happy to see him nevertheless. He had been a great help to Mike with his memory and trying to cope with the changes he experienced, even though Mike still could not remember where he was during the months he went missing.

"Good morning, Doc. How are you?" Mike said as he opened the door.

Dr. Trumbull walked through the doorway as he shook Mike's hand, looking Melissa's way to greet her also.

"I hope I'm not disturbing you guys as I usually call first, but I have some interesting news for you."

"Nah, we were just getting ready to go for a walk," Mike replied as he caught Melissa smiling.

Dr. Trumbull sat down and put his briefcase on the floor while Mike and Melissa both sat on the couch across from him.

"So, what's the interesting news?"

"Well, first I wanted you to know that Phil Grant is recovered and back to work. I spoke with him this morning as he was curious as to how you two were doing."

Mike looked relieved.

"That's great, but doesn't he speak to Agent Durham? I mean, since our incident with Lance Prescott and the FBI's investigation of what happened to us and all."

"Oh, no, he gets all those reports and reviews everything, as he is still the agent for both of you. I think he wanted to know more on a personal basis."

"You mean from a psychological perspective."

"Well, more like a professional friendly basis. The man really cares about your well-being."

Melissa and Mike both looked at each other as Melissa said, "Aw, that's sweet of him."

Mike just smiled and asked, "So, what did you tell him?"

"The professional truth is all."

"And that would be..." Mike asked, dragging out his words as he raised both hands for an answer.

"I feel you both have adjusted exceptionally well to what happened and its outcome." He then turned his attention completely to Mike and continued. "You and I have a while to go yet to resolve some issues of memory and to help you control your amazing abilities you somehow acquired."

Mike grunted slightly before replying. "Oh, I don't know, I think I'm doing just fine in that department."

"I agree you are but the more we look at them the more we discover that we don't really know the extent of your abilities or how you came to acquire them."

"So, what's the plan, Doc?"

"The plan? I really don't have a set one except to continue doing what we're doing, as long as it's alright with you and the FBI."

"I don't think the FBI cares too much about me in that respect. I think they just want to make sure Melissa and I are safely tucked away in their program."

Judging by the look on his face, Mike felt the doctor had more to say, but was cautiously quiet.

"I have the feeling you know something else that you're not ready to tell us," Mike said.

Dr. Trumbull got up and walked to the sliding glass door and its beautiful view of the ocean.

"You guys sure lucked out with this place. It's like being on vacation all the time."

Mike and Melissa both looked at each other sensing the other shoe was about to drop and they might not like what they were going to hear. Mike was about to ask again when the doorbell rang for a second time that morning.

This time Melissa went to the door, peeked through the peephole and said, "Oh my God, it's Agent Grant!"

She opened the door and grabbed his hand and gave him a small peck on the cheek.

Phil was noticeably taken aback by her friendliness and couldn't help but blush slightly.

"Uh, hi. How is everybody?" he said as he walked halfway through the door before realizing that they were not alone.

"Dr. Trumbull, I wasn't expecting you here."

"Well, no, I wasn't scheduled for today, but I thought under the circumstances it might not be a bad idea to show up."

Mike and Melissa both looked at each other, the concern on their faces made Agent Grant smirk and look up in the air as he made his way to Mike to shake his hand.

"Mike, you're looking well. I hope you and Melissa have settled in and like your new digs." As he said this and before Mike could answer, Melissa chimed in, "Yeah, it's really nice here. We both love the solitude that the beach offers."

"Yes, but sooner or later I should look for some kind of work. Don't you think?" Mike added.

Mike and Melissa both sat back down on the couch, still

glancing at each other in anticipation of what Dr. Trumbull meant by his comment. Agent Grant moved to one of the chairs and motioned for the doctor to sit on the other chair.

"You're both probably wondering what the good doctor meant by his comment, and I was kind of hoping that I could have seen the two of you before the doctor did, but I guess..." Before Phil could continue, Dr. Trumbull interrupted.

"Agent Grant, I didn't say anything to them yet."

Phil had a look of surprise and then disappointment as he realized that he had just ruined the way he had hoped to speak to Mike and Melissa about why he had come.

"Terrific. Okay, well look, I guess I blew that one," he said as he adjusted in the chair.

"What is going on?" Mike asked.

"As you know, I've been following Mike's progress with the doctor, reading all the reports and discussing them with my superiors. They all like what they see. But specifically, they like the things that Mike is capable of."

Mike developed a look of concern on his face as he reached for Melissa's hand.

"What do you mean, exactly?"

Before Phil could answer, Dr. Trumbull said, "I think he's referring to your telekinetic abilities."

"What, they think I'm some kind of freak or something?"

"No, no, nothing like that," Phil said.

"They realize that you're very special and suggested that I approach you with a proposal of sorts."

"What kind of proposal?" Melissa asked.

Agent Grant looked at the doctor as if to say, "Okay, your turn," and the doctor obliged.

"I think what Agent Grant is trying to tell you is that the FBI, knowing that you possess certain abilities far above anyone else, would like to know if you would use them for the betterment of society."

Mike looked at Melissa and halfway smiled, shaking his head and said, "You mean like offering me a job?"

"Exactly," Phil said.

Mike got up off the couch and walked over to the window, staring out at the ocean and the serene view that it offered. Melissa got up and walked over next to him and whispered in his ear.

"You're the one who said you should look for work." Mike turned around to face Agent Grant and the doctor.

"I don't know what to say. I mean, how would that work, and am I ready for something like that?"

"There would be a lot of training involved and I want you to know that it might not be easy, but I've spoken with the good doctor here, who thinks you can do it."

As he said this, he looked at Dr. Trumbull who looked at Mike and said, "And I want you to know that I'll be available for you whenever you need me."

Mike turned to face Melissa and held both her hands and asked, "How do you feel about this, honey?"

"I believe in you. You're a good man with strong convictions and whatever you decide is fine with me."

Mike looked out the window one more time before replying. "Let me think on it a bit, would you?"

Phil got up from the chair and walked over to Mike and offered his hand. As the two of them shook, Phil said, "I understand, you and Melissa discuss it more and I'll wait for your answer."

Later in the day, with the sun setting to the rhythmic sound of the waves as they crashed along the shoreline, Mike and Melissa lay on their deck, sipping wine and listened to the haunting cry of the seagulls as they sang their lonely song. She glanced at him and as their eyes met. He could hear her voice in his head as she thought, *I love you*. As long as that was true, that was all he really needed. When their glasses were empty, Mike reached out his hand to grab the bottle of Cabernet Sauvignon as it floated from the nearby table to his hand.

"See, honey," he said, "as long as you love me, I can do anything."

She knew what he meant, just as she knew he would accept Agent Grant's offer.

The End

Printed in the United States
219412BV00002B/6/P